TEMPTATION

When we got to my house, he stopped the motor and took me in his arms. I'd be lying if I said it didn't feel nice, being enfolded in his arms and smelling that nice kind of burning-pine-needles scent that seems to hover around his collarbone.

"Please, please, Robin," he whispered, his lips brushing my hair. "I want you to be my girl. *Really* be my girl." Of course I knew what he meant by *really*...

Other Avon Flare Books by
Norma Howe

GOD, THE UNIVERSE AND HOT FUDGE SUNDAES

IN WITH THE OUT CROWD

NORMA HOWE

AN AVON FLARE BOOK

AVON BOOKS
A division of
The Hearst Corporation
105 Madison Avenue
New York, New York 10016

Copyright © 1986 by Norma Howe
Published by arrangement with Houghton Mifflin Company
Library of Congress Catalog Card Number: 86-10346
ISBN: 0-380-70472-2
RL: 5.4

First Avon Flare Printing: January 1988

AVON FLARE TRADEMARK REG. U.S. PAT. OFF. AND IN OTHER COUNTRIES.
MARCA REGISTRADA. HECHO EN U.S.A.

Printed in the U.S.A.

K-R 10 9 8 7 6 5 4 3 2 1

For THE WEREWOLF —
and friends

IN WITH THE OUT CROWD

1

The bell has long since rung in my English Lit class, so that means Mr. Wallace is late again. Some of the kids are starting to act up, but I sit quietly at my desk by the chalkboard. I just sit here like a big nothing and watch passively as handsome, blond Bill Conyers, varsity quarterback and team captain, deliberately opens April Maye's purse and threatens to empty its contents out of the window, piece by piece.

April screams bloody murder and makes a hopelessly foolish attempt to grab his arm. Bill, shrugging her off like a gnat, reaches into the purse and comes up with her lipstick. He holds it between his thumb and forefinger and leans the top half of his body out the window. "Bombs away!" he laughs.

It's hard to believe that a few weeks ago it could have been me there, having all that fun, screaming like a banshee while watching my purse being emptied out the window. All I would have had to do was say yes to Bill Conyers at Liz Altman's party.

Good old Bill. He's been after me since the eighth grade. I'm not exactly sure what he sees in me, but I guess it's something he can't help, because he told me once that he had me "under his skin." We were sitting in his brother's Pinto by the lake in Fields Park one night, and he was holding my hand and running it up and down his arm and that's when he said it. It's hard not to like somebody who tells you that.

Liz Altman's parents were away the Friday night Liz had her party, and Bill had led me out to a little sundeck off the master bedroom. I felt funny walking through Liz's parents' room like that — smelling her mother's perfume and everything — but the door wasn't locked, and Bill seemed to know the way.

At first we just sat together on the padded lounge chair on the sundeck, and Bill started off by kissing me in that leisurely way of his. But soon there was that new kind of intensity in his face and in the way he pushed me down on the lounge chair and moved his body up close to mine.

I think what saved me that night was the bug zapper. Bill was snuggling up, getting real cozy, but all the while I kept hearing little sizzling sounds from the back of the brick planter. Every few seconds, at irregular intervals, I'd hear a click and then a sizzle. Sometimes the sizzle would last for a pretty long time, and I'd envision a really big fat moth getting electrocuted in there, flaming up like a birthday candle. It seemed almost symbolic to me, and after a little while I sat back up and told Bill we'd better stop it.

He was pretty mad, I guess, and later, on the way home, he started quoting all those statistics to me again, pointing out that half of all sixteen-year-olds have already done it, and there was obviously something very wrong (cold and unloving) with me.

Well, I didn't have any problem believing his statistics. I know for certain April Maye has already been checked off, and even Jennifer *says* she has, and maybe she really has. But something kept holding me back — I'm not quite sure what.

When we got to my house, he stopped the motor and took me in his arms again. I'd be lying if I said it didn't feel nice, being enfolded in his arms and smelling that nice kind of burning-pine-needles scent that seems to hover around his collarbone.

"Please, please, Robin," he whispered, his lips brushing my hair. "I want you to be my girl. *Really* be my girl." Of course, I knew what he meant by that *really*.

Oh boy, it was tempting, though. And not just for the momentary thrill of it, either; all it would have taken to put me right in the center of my crowd again, and not just the tag-along I had gradually become, was simply to have said yes to Bill that night.

The next day, when Jennifer called to rehash the party, I cupped my hands around the phone and told her how close I had come to becoming another teenage statistic. I tried to be funny about it, even mentioning the bug

3

zapper, but Jennifer didn't think it was funny at all. She just sighed and said I was really stupid to turn down a guy as nice and as popular as Bill, and what was the matter with me lately, anyway.

"Eeekkk!" April is screaming again. "Bill! You stop that!"

Her yellow comb is next. Bill examines it briefly and then tosses it out the window like an orange peel. A couple of kids get out of their seats and wander over to watch the fun from a more advantageous viewing point.

"You'd better give me that!" April threatens again, making a futile lurch for her purse. I don't mean to be nasty, but somehow I have the feeling April will have no problem at all doing what's expected of her if she really wants to be Bill's girl. Really.

"Quit that!" she screams. But she doesn't fool this cookie for a moment; she's having the time of her life. She's been after Bill for years, and now it looks as though she may be succeeding at last.

Bill quickly glances my way, and I suddenly see in those darting blue eyes a flash of that indefinable something, that hardness and inflexibility that somehow keeps me from loving him. I'm no expert on love, of course, but I'm pretty sure that when you're truly in love, those nagging little doubts — like I have about Bill — just don't keep getting in the way. As much as I long to fit in again, as much as I dread becoming one of those dreary kids who don't belong, I know in my heart I'm not ready to pay the price. Try as I might, I just can't allow myself to give in to Bill, even though he gets better looking with each passing week and is the most popular guy in the most popular crowd in school.

I sigh and reach into my bookbag and fish out our assigned paperback, Hawthorne's *The Scarlet Letter*, and flip to page 35, where I left off last night.

We are supposed to begin reading it next week, over Christmas vacation, but I don't see any harm in starting it early. Besides, I don't have anything else to do; nobody has called me on the phone, not even Jennifer. Where my friends are concerned, things are really starting to go to hell in a handbasket, as far as I can see.

Just now another ear-piercing scream comes from over by the windows. Bill has just thrown April's wallet across the room to Mike Soto. Besides her cigarettes, something very personal has fallen out, and they start throwing *that* around.

I'm in no mood for all that foolishness. I don't know what's gotten into me lately. It seems to me that my friends are acting more and more like a bunch of seven-year-olds every day, but they keep telling *me* to grow up. I just wish I could go over to that window and heave them both overboard.

"Hey, cool it!" Bob Myers says loudly. "Here comes Wallace." Bob Myers is a nerd. Nobody pays any attention to him.

Mr. Wallace enters the room on his gingerly little feet, like some mystic guru walking over a bed of hot coals. You can tell it's Mr. Wallace by the 1920s slicked-down hair, smooth ruddy cheeks, and thoroughly wimpy demeanor. Once I was complaining to my older brother,

Jamie, about what a really terrible teacher Mr. Wallace is, and Jamie just laughed and said he knew what I meant. Jamie suggested that maybe the school board had hired him just to make all the other teachers look good.

Mr. Wallace nimbly crosses over to his desk, ignoring the screams and flying objects, and suddenly opens his suit coat like a skid row flasher. I can't believe it: pinned to the front of his shirt is a gaudy letter *A*, cut from red felt and adorned with stitched-in curlicues.

Actually, Mr. Wallace never wanted to be a teacher at all. Self-conscious and withdrawn, he would have preferred to be an antiquities librarian or, in his wildest fantasies, a Buddhist monk. At least that's what he told my father last Parents' Night.

My father has never missed a Parents' Night in all my years of school. When called upon, my father plays the part of the perfect father. The thing with my father is that he thinks he's in the movies. It's the longest-running movie in history. It's been going on for thirty-nine years now. My father's always playing some part or other. But I guess there's nothing wrong with it, if that's the part he wants to play.

My father and mother met through my aunt Tracy, Mom's sister. She's dead now. Her name was Tracy Boyd, but everyone called her Spacey. My mother doesn't like to talk about her much, and my dad won't talk about her at all. Apparently she was a real loner, and she drove my grandmother Boyd crazy with her moody and independent ways. My mom says she just never fit in with the crowd and was always distant and aloof, wearing weird clothes like ponchos and army fatigues long before they came into style. She absolutely refused to attend the Cotillion Ball, and that infuriated my grandmother so much, she practically disowned her.

Grandmother Boyd is a very conservative person who lives in Pasadena. She hates people on welfare, men with beards, and young ladies dressed in fatigues. To this day she doesn't understand how she could have given birth to somebody like Spacey. I mean Tracy. But life seems to be full of little surprises like that.

Tracy and my dad met at a campground in Yosemite the summer after Dad graduated from high school. He was there with a bunch of his friends, but Tracy, typically, was on her own, working part time at the camp cafeteria and spending her free time wandering around the hiking trails. They had a whirlwind romance that lasted for three weeks. My mom told me that, for Tracy, it was some kind of record. When the summer was over, my dad stopped by Tracy's house to pick up his high school ring, which he had impulsively given to her at the height of their affair, and that's when he met Mom. They found out they were both headed for Berkeley that fall and arranged to look each other up. The rest is history.

During their first year, they lived together more or less clandestinely — as people away at college can do — and by their second year they had decided to tie the knot. My mother, a pioneering feminist wanting to make a statement, insisted on a hyphenated name. But they didn't know whose name should go before the hyphen and whose after. Most people think there's a rule about that, but nobody seems to know what it is. They called the marriage license bureau, and the clerk there said heck, she didn't care, do whatever they wanted. So, with a flip of a coin, Ilene Boyd and Blinky Tweedy became Mr. and Mrs. Tweedy-Boyd. In no time at all they had a baby boy they named Jamie to juggle back and forth between classes.

The Tweedy-Boyds really applied themselves and received their degrees the month after I was born. They went back to Southern California, toting little me in the bassinet that had once been Jamie's, and moved into the house next door to my father's parents: that would be my grandfather (whom we called Muncie, after his hometown) and my grandma Noddy. My dad got a dream job (for him) managing a drive-in theater, my mother started law school, and Grandma Noddy took care of Jamie and me while our parents were away. All in all, it was an ideal arrangement.

Meanwhile, Tracy had gotten herself involved with some far-out quasi-religious sect based in Switzerland called Conscious-You'nme and went over there and became a "none." She sent a little mimeographed pamphlet to my grandmother Boyd once asking for money (one of her few communications home), and that's how we learned what the You'nmes call their female converts — nones.

About a year ago, on a dreary November morning, our phone rang at five minutes after seven. I was in the bathroom getting ready for school and came out just as my mom was hanging up the receiver. "That was long distance from Switzerland," she said slowly, tracing over the notes she had written on the pad, as if she didn't believe her own writing.

What had happened was that Tracy had suffered an attack of appendicitis and they couldn't get her down off the mountain and to a doctor in time. My grandmother had her body sent home and she was buried at Mount Vernon Cemetery, which is about five miles from our house. My father presided at the funeral, playing the part of a bereaved relative, glossing over her shortcomings and excusing her faults. When he concluded, referring to her as "a lovely free spirit, home at last," everyone cried. I looked at Grandmother Boyd then, and even though her expression was pained and her eyes were moist, I could tell by a certain set of her mouth that she could never forgive her daughter Tracy for breaking the conservative family mold.

Later that night, after everyone else had gone to bed, my mother and I were sitting alone in the dining room, talking about Tracy. Grandmother Boyd had given Mom a big box of Tracy's things that she had been saving, and Mom and I had been going through it. There was a professional photograph of Tracy, wearing a peasant blouse and a delicate gold necklace.

"She was sixteen when this was taken," Mom said. "Just your age." She shook her head. "Such a strange little person. Always reading mystery stories and fantasies instead of doing her homework." Mom made a pitiful little smile and wrinkled her brows. "Gosh, how your grandmother Boyd would nag and get after her about that. Sometimes I think all that nagging just made the problem worse. It got to be a battle of wills after a while."

Mom studied the photograph a little longer, then handed it to me. "By the time this was taken," she said softly, "Tracy was turning into a real loner. She just couldn't seem to keep a friendship going for any length of time — and that went for girls as well as boys. I think the biggest problem was that she just didn't seem to really care about anyone. Except herself, of course." Mom's voice dropped almost to a whisper. "Do you know what I mean? She just couldn't seem to love anyone, to give herself to anyone. In the end, all she thought about was herself."

After Mom went to bed, I took Tracy's photograph into my room and went over to the mirror. There was something about her that reminded me a little of myself. I studied the picture some more, and I noticed that we resembled each other mostly around the eyes. Dark brown and set far apart, they could easily have been interchanged without detection. Her hair was long and parted simply in the middle. Mom said that was the style back then. My own hair is much shorter, parted on the side and done in a layered cut. I ducked my head forward and combed my hair down straight over my eyes and parted it in the middle, like Tracy's. Since it was so short on the sides, I cupped my hands around my ears and tried to picture how I'd look with long hair. I looked so much like Tracy I couldn't believe it.

How else were we alike? If I resembled her on the outside, I wondered, how much was I like her on the inside?

2

As an attention-getting device, the red *A* is surprisingly effective.

"Get a load of Mr. Wallace!" Mike Soto exclaims from the rear of the classroom.

"Hey! Where did you get that, Mr. Wallace? Did you embroidery that yourself?"

"Embroider, stupid!" someone says. " 'Embroidery that yourself.' God, what an illiterate moron!"

"All right, class," Mr. Wallace says after clearing his throat several times. "Let's settle down now."

We settle down, but slowly, like a boiling pot of fudge when you remove it from the heat. We don't settle down because Mr. Wallace told us to, though. We settle down because of our vice-principal, a certain Mr. James Bussone, better known as "The Buzzard." It is safe to say that Mr. Bussone is the most universally hated person on

11

this campus. He's only been here for two years, and during that time he has not only canceled our Festival Day (he said there was "covert drinking") but also was responsible for closing the campus at noon (the neighbors were complaining about the mess and noise), discontinuing Friday afternoon rallies during classtime (he said to have them after school and see how many kids showed up then), forbidding the traditional Senior Ditch Day (the school was losing money from the state for unexcused absences), and harassing Senior Rally, a "club" for selected senior girls.

When my dad's twin brother, Uncle Wink, told me that Mr. Bussone was one of his old college buddies, I was sure it must have been a case of mistaken identity. I just couldn't picture the Buzzard ever being anybody's buddy, except maybe Dracula's.

All eyes are on Mr. Wallace now and the fancy red *A* pinned to his shirt. It's very obvious that he's mighty pleased with himself. I can just imagine him thinking, Ha! A little planning and I've got the slimy little savages right in the palm of my hand.

He points to his chest. "So, class, what does this red letter *A* stand for? Does anyone know?"

Talk about stupid questions. Of course everyone knows. At least we know *that* much about *The Scarlet Letter*. There is a scattering of giggles and a few hands shoot up. But before Mr. Wallace can call on anyone, Mike Soto cups his hands around his mouth and calls out gruffly, "Uh, how about *abnormal*, Mr. Wallace?"

The rest of the class pounds their desks and roars with laughter.

Mr. Wallace pretends to join in the merriment at first, but I think I can spot a broken heart when I see one. In this instance, I can see the blood slowly oozing out and staining his nice white shirt. I can even read his mind. He's thinking, this is third period; I've got four more periods to go today, plus lunch, and then there's twenty-one more weeks before summer, and thirty-one more years until I can retire and move to Timbuktu.

He gazes at us in his silly trancelike way and waits until we quiet down. Then he suddenly gets very maudlin. "You know, people," he says in his misery, looking at the grinning faces before him, "these years — these precious high school years — you'll find as you grow older, you'll look back on these years and realize that they were the happiest years of your life."

I look up in shocked surprise. My God, is he kidding? If that's true, I think, I may as well just throw in the old towel and end it all, right here and now.

I glance quickly around the room. Everyone else seems normal and happy, relishing the happiest years of their lives. What's wrong with me, anyway?

The period ends and something happens to make me realize I am not alone. As Emery Day files past me on his way to the door, he reaches out and touches me lightly on the elbow. Emery Day — short, splattered with pimples, a first-class gold medal nobody — touches my elbow and gives me a rueful little smile. "I think I'm going to cut next period," he says very softly, "and go home and hang myself in the closet."

I've known Emery Day since kindergarten days. He was two weeks late. By the time he arrived, all the other kids knew how to salute the flag and where to find their colors.

Miss Wooliscroft made a big deal out of the fact that "we have a new little boy with us this morning."

The new little boy had carrot-red hair and white, white skin. His face looked like a cheese cake freshly sprinkled with graham cracker crumbs, and his ears stuck out like sails. He was wearing striped overalls and ankle-high boots, and with that red hair and beaklike nose, he looked more like a three-foot-tall parrot than a kindergarten kid.

"Boys and girls," Miss Wooliscroft said, "this is Emery Day."

Emery's face turned so red that pretty soon you couldn't tell where his face left off and his hair began. Then he stood on the outsides of his boots, teetering there, until Miss Wooliscroft had to hike him up by the collar and tell him to stand up straight like a little man. For some not too obscure reason, the kids all started to laugh.

When we saluted the flag, he just stood there like a dummy. And then he went to the girls' lavatory. Emery Day had a very bad start.

He continued to wear overalls until the fourth grade, when he switched to jeans. But they were all wrong. I think his mother used to get them at the Woolco. They were about a foot too long, so he had folded them over

14

several times, all lopsided. Usually they would come un-
folded and he'd trip on them. Emery was always the last
one to be chosen — for everything.

I can't remember if he started crying before or after the
big switch to jeans, but it was at about that time. Emery
would cry in school a couple of times a week. At first the
kids used to tease him about it, but then it kind of got
to be old hat. Pretty soon nobody seemed to worry much
about it anymore. One day, though, I felt so sorry for
him crying there at his seat that I offered him a handful
of red hots. But Mrs. Stafford caught me and we both
got in trouble. We had to be last in the cafeteria line for
the next two weeks.

The cafeteria supervisor was named Mrs. Findley, and
she ruled over us with an iron fist. She posted herself
next to the milk cooler and, armed with a policeman's
whistle, saw to it that we conducted ourselves like little
robots. Being next to Emery in line meant that I sat next
to him at the table, too, since getting out of line was a
capital offense. Because Mrs. Findley allowed a mini-
mum of conversation ("You're here to *eat*, children, not
talk!"), Emery and I started writing little notes to each
other on our napkins, mostly derogatory comments about
Mrs. Findley's hair, posture, and ankle socks.

But after the two weeks' punishment was over, I went
back to my usual place with my regular friends.

My regular friends were all kids from the Three Oaks
Swim and Tennis Club. My parents were charter members at Three Oaks, since it was organized the same year

I started school. I really loved that place. It was near our house (it still is), and Jamie with his crowd and I with mine spent long, lazy summer days over there, swimming and lying around in the sun. By September, we were always as brown and freckled as the chocolate chip cookies they sold in the snack bar.

Jennifer's family were charter members at Three Oaks, too, and Jennifer became my special friend right from the start. We really came to depend upon one another during those early days. That was when her parents started divorce proceedings (her mother has since remarried), and my dad's long-smoldering drinking problem finally surfaced. Jennifer practically lived with us that particular summer while her mother was going through those personal problems, and it was during that time that I was awakened one night by a loud argument and overheard my mother giving my father an ultimatum: either he would give up his drinking or she would take us kids and leave him. After the worst month of my life, Dad finally admitted he was an alcoholic and joined AA. (He hasn't touched the stuff since, thank God.) I know I'll always remember how Jennifer and I would whisper our deepest fears to one another in the semidarkness of my room, crying unashamedly together and vowing eternal friendship, no matter what happened. I don't know what I would have done without her, and I'm sure it was the same for her. That summer our parents sent us to camp together near Big Bear for three weeks, and we solemnly exchanged the beaded Indian friendship rings we made in crafts. I still have mine in a miniature cedar chest with hand-painted violets on the lid. I don't know what Jennifer did with hers.

The Conyers and the Monroes and the Altmans all joined Three Oaks at about that time. Lynnie Jeffries moved to town when we were in the fifth grade, and after inquiring around her family joined too. It was a sure way aware parents had of seeing that their kids would have easy access to the "right kind" of friends. Take Muriel, for example. Her father is a dermatologist and wanted to make sure his shy little daughter wouldn't get lost in the shuffle. If she weren't a member and always around, we'd probably not even know she was alive. So now she's still a member of the group, even though her chief function is to sit on the end whenever we're all together.

The year we were in the fifth grade was the happiest time of my whole life. We got a new swimming coach at Three Oaks that year with whom we all fell in love. He was this college kid named Oscar Overfelt, but we all called him Ozzie. If Ozzie had asked us to jump in the water with our feet in cement blocks and plastic bags over our heads, we would have done it, with ribbons. The girls all swooned over him, and the boys tried to be like him.

Ol' Ozzie was the picture of health and would always try to impress upon us the importance of clean living. He'd have this little routine where he'd holler, "Are Ozzie's kids going to eat too much sugar and ruin their teeth?" And we'd all yell back, "No!" Then he'd say, "Are Ozzie's kids going to watch TV until midnight and not get their eight hours of shut-eye?" We'd yell back even louder, "No, no!" Then, "Are Ozzie's kids going to smoke cigarettes and ruin their bodies?" That's when we'd answer in chorus, "No, no, a million times no!"

The kids elected me captain of the twelve-and-under swimming team that year, and we won the city championship. I still have a string of blue ribbons on my wall to remind me of those wonderful days. The last time Jennifer was in my room, she remarked on the ribbons. "My God," she said, "do you still have those things around? I threw mine out a long time ago."

I don't know what Emery Day did all summer. There were plenty of kids who weren't Three Oakers, and they didn't count for beans.

April Maye doesn't wait for me after English class (what else is new?) so I decide to stop at my locker on the way to the cafeteria and dump off some stuff. We have a closed campus at my school. That means you can't escape, even for lunch. You're virtually a prisoner from eight-thirty till three o'clock for 181 days of the year.

I fool around at my locker longer than I need to and finally walk toward the cafeteria with a vague feeling of dread. The thing is, I think I'm in the process of losing the friends I've had for years, and I don't know if it's their fault or mine. I've noticed it coming on for months now, but I just can't explain what's happening. I'm no prude (I don't think!), but I don't really feel comfortable with a lot of things they're doing — and they know it — but still I keep hanging around, pretending that everything is the same as it's always been.

Making new friends is just out of the question, because the sad truth is that my years with the in crowd have turned me into a snob. A reluctant snob, maybe, but a snob's a snob, and it's embarrassing and difficult to try to make friends with kids whom you've ridiculed and made fun of in the past. And we do make fun of them. We make fun of the things they say or don't say, the things they do or don't do, the way they dress and the way they look. We rate them mercilessly with our intricate double-digit rating system. We call them fringe-freaks and near-nerds and rake them over the coals from 1 to 10 and from A to Z and back again.

All the double-A tens are already sitting at our table after I go through the food line with my tray. If they want to, they can make room for me. I feel kind of sick but decide I'll chance it. It's either that or sitting alone.

I sidle up between Jennifer (still my best bet) and Michelle Rutherford. Michelle is the newest addition to our table and her standing is still on the shaky side.

"Oh, hi, Robin," Jennifer says not especially enthusiastically. She nudges Michelle. "Hey, move it, Michelle."

I step over the bench and sit down between them. Nobody else seems to notice me. They are deeply involved in the pastime of the hour — making up outrageous bumper stickers on the subject of how certain segments of society do it.

"Shoeshine boys do it with polish!" Randi says to the moans and groans of everyone. Randi's specialty was the breast stroke during that golden summer. You can still see the effects of it. She quit going to Three Oaks last year when her parents finally got their own pool. The Jeffries family quit then, too, since Lynnie started going to Randi's pool all the time. I don't care, though. It doesn't matter anymore.

"How about, singers do it with glee!" Jennifer says.

"I don't get it," April Maye says, staring her down.

"Glee club, you nerd. Singers, glee club. Get it now?" Jennifer is glaring back at her, holding her own.

"Yeah, I guess so," April says, turning away. "But it's not funny."

"Paramedics do it in an emergency," Muriel Monroe pipes up in her thin little voice.

"You didn't just make that up, Muriel. I saw that yesterday on a Toyota pickup."

"Oh yes I did! I didn't see that on any Toyota pickup."

"Oh yeah? Tell me about it, Muriel."

"Hey, you guys, how about this?" April breaks in with her breathy stage whisper.

We all lean forward to catch every word of her priceless gem.

"Housewives do it with a lick and a promise!"

Screams and laughter explode from our table as we lean back like a flower bursting into bloom. But, for me, it's another one of those awful moments when two opposing forces seem to be pulling from opposite directions. Outwardly I'm laughing with the crowd, but inwardly I'm ashamed of myself.

It seems as though everyone else in the cafeteria pauses

to stare at us, no doubt wondering what the ins are laughing at now.

"God, April," Randi says admiringly after she has finally straightened up from her laughing fit. "That's gross!"

That's exactly what I think, too. Gross is the word, and I'm getting sick of grossness.

After lunch we stack our trays and split up. Jennifer and I go to gym together, and the other kids go their separate ways until we meet again in sixth period for our drama class. Gym is the only class Jennifer and I have together without any of the other kids.

"God, Robin," she says as we make our way across the playing field, "you really blew it when you turned Bill down, you know that? Now April's starting to make a big play for him, as you've probably noticed."

I sigh and stare at the ground as we walk. "You're not going to bring that up again, are you? I sure wish you'd change the record."

"But I just don't *get* it," she says. "Nobody turns Bill down. It's like . . . like" — she gropes — "well, it's sort of like inviting all your friends to your suicide, don't you see?"

"No. I don't see that at all."

"Okay, well, inviting your friends to your suicide, that would be like *flaunting* life, see? And that's just what you did. You flaunted Bill, and that means you flaunted us, too."

"Flaunted?" I mimic. "If you mean *flouted*, why don't you say so?"

"You know what I mean!" Jennifer answers angrily as her cheeks flush bright red. "And see how you do? That's a good example right there of how you're acting lately. Like you're too good for us anymore."

"How can I be too good for you?" I ask icily before I can stop myself. "How can I be too good for the best crowd in school?"

Jennifer sets her lips in a tight little line and just stares at me.

I know right away I have gone too far. "I'm sorry, Jennifer," I say finally as we walk up the steps to the gym. "I'm sorry. It's just that with Bill, well, I just didn't want to . . ." I falter.

Jennifer looks disgusted. "I know very well what you *didn't want* to do. You can't even say it, for God's sake. Listen, Robin, we're not in the fifth grade anymore. Everything's changed. *We've* changed."

"You can say that again," I mutter.

"See there," she says accusingly. "That's just what I'm talking about. I'm telling you, Robin, no one's going to want to have anything to do with you unless you quit acting so judgmental. You just seem to be passing judgment on us all the time."

"I'm not passing judgment," I answer quietly, but I know that's exactly what I'm doing.

She shakes her head. I notice her pained expression. "I . . . I still like you, Robin," she says with a slight hesitation, and for the first time I wonder if she still really means that. "But," she continues, "there's still this thing with Bill. He's really upset with you, you know. He . . . he told me he's getting really fed up with that good-little-girl act of yours."

"It's not an act," I begin, but Jennifer doesn't hear.

"I don't know how much longer I can stick up for you," she's saying, "and that's the truth. So just quit passing judgment, will you, or I'm warning you, the kids are going to turn on you, starting with Bill."

Something about the way she says Bill's name makes me look up quickly, but her eyes shift away from me. "What do you mean?" I ask, starting to take her arm. She shakes me off gently and heads toward her gym locker, leaving me standing with my arm outstretched toward her.

The old Three Oaks gang stayed pretty much a closed group during our first year (sixth grade) at Wilson Middle School. Jennifer and I and three or four of the other girls were all in the same homeroom. Bill and Lynnie and some of those kids were in a different one, but we all got together at lunchtime. Until the rainy weather started, we all boycotted the cafeteria and brought bag lunches. Then we'd sit in this big circle under the palm trees near the school parking lot, laughing and joking and singing and fooling around, making all the out kids wish to high heaven they were in.

The only thing I remember about Emery Day during all that time is that he was picked once as the Lions Club Student of the Month, and none of us could figure out why. Not that we really cared, except that all the student leaders came from our ranks, and he was sure not one of us.

April Maye arrived at Wilson Middle School during our second year and caused a major explosion. She was fresh from some kind of private boarding school back East and was like a strobe light in a candle factory. She became a focal point, bringing together the "best" kids from all three elementary schools that fed into Wilson. Jennifer and I, of course, were right in the thick of it.

I had my first real run-in with April at a slumber party at her house. After her parents had gone to bed, she disappeared into the kitchen for a minute and came back with a gallon of red wine.

"The hard stuff is all locked up and they're all out of white," she said, "but this stuff will be okay."

Someone got some paper cups from the bathroom and we all started "swiggin' the booze," as April laughingly said. I didn't drink a whole lot, but I went along with it. We all felt so wild and grown up.

Then April lit a cigarette. I'll never forget it. It was a Virginia Slims. Something deep inside me rebelled, but at first I wasn't sure what it was. April passed the pack around, and as I reached for one I remembered. I carefully put the cigarette back in the pack and recited loudly, knowing for certain that the others would join in, "No, no, a million times no!"

There were a few nervous laughs from former Three Oakers and some blank stares from the newcomers. "Oh,

Robin," Lynnie said, watching April and sticking a cigarette in her mouth, "why don't you grow up?"

The whole room was suddenly quiet while everyone waited to see what would happen. Jennifer didn't take a cigarette, and neither did Muriel and two or three of the others, but most of the kids took one and lit right up with April.

That April knew exactly what was going on. She looked at Jennifer and then at me and did a little trick expression that I've come to detest. What she did was a series of quick little fake smiles, keeping her mouth closed and just raising the corners of it in fast little jerks. The whole routine lasted only a second or two, but the power struggle that began that night, though waxing and waning throughout the years, has lasted to this day.

3

Sixth-period drama class was a lot of fun for the first couple of weeks of the semester. Mrs. Madison is young and enthusiastic and taught us a lot about the basics of drama. It was Jennifer's idea that we all take it together as an elective. Emery Day is in that class, too. I have no idea what he is doing there, especially since he's a senior now. As I said, I kind of lost track of him for a while in middle school, and when I started high school, I found out that he had been taking classes in the summers and skipped the eighth grade.

The first play we read was *You Can't Take It with You.* Mrs. Madison could barely contain her delight at the madcap family depicted in the play.

"Can you imagine," she asked, stifling a giggle and gesturing wildly with fluttering fingers, "making firecrackers in the basement, ballet dancing all through the house?" She smiled right at me then, with wet and shiny eyes, but I could only look up at the ceiling, picturing my own crazy family, and think, *Big deal*.

Mrs. Madison must have caught my expression. "You don't agree, Robin?"

"Pardon me?"

"You don't agree that this is a rather unusual family, here in the play?"

"Oh, yes, I agree," I answered. "They're unusual, all right." But in the back of my mind I was comparing the firecracker inventor and the ballet dancer to my own family, and the people in the play seemed like a bunch of bores.

I've already explained a little about my father, the pseudo movie star and reformed alcoholic. My mother, of course, is a lawyer. Her main specialty is women's rights — sexual harassment and things like that. Sexual harassment is very popular right now. But she's also a gung-ho animal lover, so she likes to represent animals in distress whenever she can, which is not too often. Her biggest victory yet in the animal department was last summer, when she won $50,000 for a female cocker spaniel named DeeDee. The relatives of a deceased old widow contested her will, which named DeeDee as chief beneficiary, but they didn't have a leg to stand on, so DeeDee got the dough.

When she got the case she's working on now, Mom thought she had died and gone to heaven, it's so much right down her alley. It's about a male Airedale named Macho whose owner boosted him over a six-foot fence so he (the Airedale) could illegally impregnate a gorgeous purebred Chow-Chow named Chinky. Mom gives us a blow-by-blow each night at dinner. All she can talk about lately is Macho and Chinky, Chinky and Macho. Apparently, their owners met at obedience school, and there was some sort of thwarted romance. At any rate, there's more involved than just the dogs. My mom had a really bad day the time one juror candidate, an Asian, made the point that he considered Chinky a racist name. My mom was sure he'd make an outstanding juror, but since he obviously would be unsympathetic toward her client (Chinky's mistress), she had to excuse him, reluctantly but fast.

"Well," my dad had said, winking broadly at us, playing the comedian, "that must have been a real chink in your armor — ho-ho-ho."

My little sister Naomi — she's nine — wiped the milk off her mouth with her sleeve. "Listen, Daddy," she said solemnly, "that's not funny. You'd better say 'a Chinese person in your armor' from now on."

My dad was miffed because she got a bigger laugh from us than he did, and she wasn't even trying to be funny.

Then there's one of my favorite people in my family — good old Uncle Wink. As far as characters are concerned, he makes the firecracker inventor in the play seem like a second-rate bit player.

Uncle Wink's a Tweedy, my dad's twin brother. But

they're not identical. Uncle Winky likes to say they're as different as two peas in a pod. Take the way they dress, for instance. My dad, well, he always goes in for the latest styles. The last time Mom cleaned out his closet, it was like a capsule review of fashion fads, from Nehru jackets to leisure suits. Uncle Wink, on the other hand, always wears the same thing — a brown suit, white shirt, and a dark brown tie. The top button of his shirt is always undone, and the tie is loosened and hanging there like a dead fish. He says he has to be prepared because he never knows where his paper is liable to send him.

Actually, Uncle Wink leads a double life. By day he is a very respected reporter specializing in science articles for the most prestigious newspaper in Southern California. He wouldn't appreciate my mentioning the name of the paper because his carefully guarded secret would be revealed: namely, by night he transforms himself into the renowned Miss Prudence Penrose Honeysuckle, celebrated authoress of a hundred and one best-selling romantic novels. Her (his) latest sensation, *Tremble Uncontrollably at Love's Sweet Call*, recounts the absorbing tale of beautiful, flaxen-haired Lady Oribel's voyage to the West Indies while being held captive in a wine barrel by the recklessly handsome Stretchford Lastic, a wealthy rubber merchant disguised as an Italian sailor.

Wink flies his own airplane and owns a boat. He is also working secretly on a unique book of photographs he is taking himself all over the country which is tentatively titled *From Screen Doors to Wine-Stained Rugs:*

Present-Day Images of Jesus. Clearly, there is more to Uncle Wink than meets the eye.

There is more to my whole family than meets the eye, but of course I didn't explain that to Mrs. Madison. Anyway, after the first couple of weeks of the semester, she got pregnant. Then she had some complications and had to take an extended leave of absence. That's when we got Mr. Alex Huntsman, a long-term substitute with a short-term brain. God, how I hate that guy.

Emery Day is standing out in the hall as I trail behind the other kids walking into the drama classroom. He's wearing his usual plaid flannel shirt and blue denim vest. There's nothing wrong with Levi vests, I suppose, but the only one in Southside High is on Emery's back.

"Hey, Emery," I say on an impulse, stopping and turning toward him, "you're still here."

He looks at me. Our eyes are at the exact same level. It's like looking into the mirror and getting a big scare.

I guess Emery is surprised that I even stop to talk to him. The kids in my crowd don't bother much with Emery.

"What?" he asks.

"You didn't cut school and go home and hang yourself in the closet."

We are the only people in the hall now. Emery knits his reddish brows and nods his head. "Yeah, well, I thought about it and then decided that Wallace is full of . . ." He stops short. "Let me put it this way," he says.

"I decided that Mr. Wallace is full of beans."

Mr. Huntsman leans out into the hall with his hand on the doorknob. "You two coming in or not?" he asks sarcastically.

"The bell hasn't rung yet, Mr. Huntsman," I say superpolitely. And under my breath I add, "You jerk."

It rings a few seconds later. Mr. Huntsman is up at his desk, busily tearing some sheets of paper into smaller pieces and whistling softly under his breath as if he knows exactly what he is doing.

"I need some help on a little project of mine today, folks," he says. "Those of you who came in after school last week to repair the stage curtain already know about this, but for the benefit of the others" — and here he kind of clears his throat in a self-conscious way, as if speaking about himself is difficult for him, which it isn't — "for the benefit of the others, let me explain that I'm taking a course in psychology this semester at State, and I need your help for a paper I'm writing on the subject of social adjustment."

He looks around the class innocently, with his eyes bugging out even more than usual. "It will only take a minute of your time, but anyone who doesn't wish to participate, raise your hand and you will be excused."

I'm tempted to raise my hand, but I look around and don't see any other hands up, so I just sigh and sink down in my seat.

"I'm going to do what's called a sociogram," he explains, holding up a dark green textbook called *Psychol-*

31

ogy: *The Science of Behavior*. "It explains all about it in here."

While he's passing the little blank papers around the class, I remember Jamie telling me once that since the teacher shortage, they're hiring long-term substitutes who don't even have credentials. Jamie didn't say they were hiring numbskulls, too, but I'm afraid that's what we've got.

"Now then," Mr. Huntsman says, sitting on the corner of his desk, all chummy, "I want you to pretend you're going to have a party. I want you to write down the names of three people in this class you'd invite to that party."

"What kind of party, Mr. Huntsman?"

"A pajama party?" Miles Litton asks, leering over at April.

"Any kind of party you wish," Mr. Huntsman answers with a smirk. "Now write. We can't spend all day on this."

Heads bend down over the papers. I think a minute, then write Jennifer Lewis, Muriel Monroe, and April Maye. I'd probably invite April to my party because April — well, April is kind of in the middle of everything. If you want a successful party, you'd better have April there.

Mr. Huntsman calls for the papers and tells us to study *As You Like It* in our textbook and we'll discuss it in a few minutes.

He takes up a piece of chalk and an eraser and erases the entire board. He's sort of fat, and all that exertion leaves him breathing like a leaky bicycle pump. Pretty soon he's drawing little circles and lines and arrows all over the board, consulting the little pieces of paper from time to time. Now, to my horror, he's writing initials in the little circles.

It doesn't take a genius to figure out who's who. April, Jennifer, Randi, and Michelle's circles are busily criss-crossed with lines and arrows. Obviously, they were each other's three choices. But somewhere down in the lower left-hand corner, standing out in its isolation, is my pitiful little circle. Only three people would ask me to a party. One of them is E.D. (Emery Day), another is M.M. (Muriel Monroe), and the other one is L.B. (Loreen Bays), a girl I hardly know, one of the outs, a shadowy figure who never speaks and hardly ever shows up in class.

My brother, Jamie, is a sophomore at UCLA this year and lives over there in a dorm. He's just taking a general course right now, but he wants to major in brains eventually. He says brain research is the new frontier. Jamie told me recently that investigators have just come up with an interesting fact about the human brain. It has to do with the human memory. It seems that the brain manufactures a special chemical or enzyme or something that has the ability to *fix* certain memories in our minds. The reason for that, he says, is that in order for our brains to operate most efficiently, they can't possibly remember everything. If they did, we'd get bogged down with things like grocery lists and last year's TV schedules. So most stuff we just forget. But on certain occasions the special

33

nerve cells that contain important information are bathed with the memory enzyme and become fixed in our minds. Some memories can last for a lifetime. I know I will never forget the sight of that chalkboard in drama class today.

I sit around for the rest of the period in a kind of daze. I'm only aware of the rapid beat of my pulse in my neck, the quickening of my breath, the embarrassment and the anger.

After class, Jennifer comes up to me and whispers that she is sorry. "I didn't know he'd put that on the *board*," she says, "and, anyway, I would have invited you fourth, Robin. Honestly."

I am too humiliated to answer her. All I can do is stare at her for a moment and walk away. On the way out I overhear her telling Muriel the same thing, and then I remember that Jennifer is planning on running for class secretary next semester, and elections are coming up after Christmas vacation.

I spend the rest of the afternoon at school in a mild state of panic. The die is cast. The ax has fallen. The last straw is laid on the camel's back. The barn door has slammed shut. What in God's name am I going to do? It's all I can do now to keep from crying.

After seventh period I head straight for my locker, intending to get my books and gym clothes and head out of there fast, thankful that it's Friday and there are two weeks of vacation ahead.

I round the corner by the music room and that's when I see him there, eating an apple and leaning against my locker. It's Bill Conyers.

I heave a big sigh and walk up to him.

"Hiya, Robin," he says.

"Hello, Bill."

"Uh, how you doin'?" he asks nonchalantly, making me wonder what he's up to now.

"Fine," I answer. "You want to move over? I'd like to get into my locker."

"Oh, sure. Sure." He moves over. "Uh, Robin, I want to talk to you about that little plastic bird. You know, that little whistling bird . . ."

Bill gave me that little plastic bird in a cage several months ago, the night of Randi's beach party. I felt really bad about that party. For one thing, I had to lie to my parents. I said it was going to be at Randi's house, when I knew all the time it was going to be at the beach. (I was grounded from beach parties after that awful night when Lynnie Jeffries's father came to check up on us and found all that beer. It's only been six months since that terrible automobile accident that killed David Watson, and our parents are still nervous about some of the kids' drinking and driving.) Anyway, I told my mother and father that Randi's parents would definitely be home. At least that part was true.

Mom and Dad say they trust me, but they really don't like me going to parties where there's alcohol and pot, and that seems to be the only kind I've been going to lately.

They've always liked Bill okay, though. He's really good around parents. He came to pick me up in his brother's pink Pinto. He stood around holding this big paper bag and talking to my dad man-to-man about catalytic converters while I was running around the house looking for my hooded sweatshirt. September evenings at the beach sometimes get a little chilly.

"Well, I guess I'm ready," I said finally.

"Where are you going?" Naomi asked. She always has to know where I'm going.

"Just a party."

"What time are you coming home?"

"What do you care? Who are you, my mother?"

"I was just wondering, that's all. Heck," she muttered.

Bill went over to where Naomi was sitting on the rug. "Here, little sis," he said. (He always calls her "little sis.") "You can take care of this for Robin until she gets home."

He whipped the paper bag up over this object he was carrying and flipped a little switch. The sound of a chirping bird filled the room. Naomi clapped her hands together and took the cage from him. A life-size yellow bird was twirling around on the perch and singing its little plastic heart out.

"It's just a little canary, for Robin," Bill said, ducking his head and smiling coyly behind raised eyebrows, ready to fend off any forthcoming protestations. Mom looked over at him and smiled benevolently.

Forty-five minutes later he was up to his old tricks, still trying to talk me into losing my virginity, this time under the wharf at Pike's Beach.

Now I start working the combination on my lock. "What about the bird?" I ask.

Bill shrugs at me helplessly. "Well, I need to borrow it back, sort of."

I jerk open the lock. "Borrow it back? What do you mean?"

"Yeah, well, borrow it back, more or less permanently." He smiles that winning smile of his. I can just picture him practicing in front of the mirror, getting it just the slightest bit lopsided. After knowing Bill, I've become very suspicious of lopsided smiles.

"Bill, what are you trying to say? Will you just come right out and *say* it!" I have a feeling I'm on the verge of tears. I'm still overwrought about what happened in Mr. Huntsman's class, and now Bill is beating around the bush again. I don't know if he's *ever* really told me his true feelings about anything. I've known him for years, but with Bill it's all just so superficial. I look him in the eye now and repeat, "Say it!"

He simply won't return my gaze. He quickly shifts his eyes away from mine and looks down the corridor toward the door. "The bird's not mine, actually," he starts explaining. "The thing is, well, it really belongs to my sister. See, I thought she didn't want it anymore, but it turns out, well, she does want it," he finishes weakly.

"Oh, I see." I pull the stuff I need out of my locker and a blue envelope falls to the floor. I know from the paper that it's a note from Jennifer. Apparently, she slipped it through the air vent in my locker.

Bill is bending down in a flash, retrieving it for me.

"Thanks," I say, and I stick it between the pages of *The Scarlet Letter*.

Bill is standing there awkwardly.

"Listen, Bill," I say, "it doesn't matter about the bird. Just come and get it."

He shuffles his feet around. "Okay. Sure. And, well, I'm sorry about that," he says.

I think maybe he's about to say something else, but he doesn't. He just waves his hand weakly and takes off down the hall. "Thanks, Robin," he calls over his shoulder. "I guess I'll come over for it sometime next week."

"Yeah, you do that," I say, but of course he doesn't hear me. Then I gather my stuff and duck out the exit behind the music room. I don't want to chance running into any of those kids who wouldn't think of inviting me to a party.

On a whim, I decide to stop at the Goodwill Thrift Store on my way home from school. It's at the shopping center just a few blocks from my house. I pick through the funky clothes awhile, but I don't see anything I like. Then I go over to look at the books. Actually, I am so depressed and upset and worried about my future without any friends that I don't know exactly what I'm doing.

The Goodwill is having its 50¢-per-bag book sale. The first bag I peek into has a nice illustrated junior library edition of *Little Women* right on top. I gave my copy to Naomi not too long ago in a fit of generosity and have never replaced it. I decide to get the whole bag without even looking to see what other books are in there.

The line at the cash register is really long, but I join it anyway. I watch the clerk finish wrapping a ton of dishes and glasses for someone who looks vaguely familiar. I finally place him. He's a vendor at the flea market. On weekends, the drive-in theater Dad manages turns into a flea market. Wink and Jamie and I used to go there sometimes on Sundays, but we haven't been going much since Jamie's been living at the dorm. Guys like that buy stuff at the Goodwill all the time and then resell it for ten times as much at the flea market, saying it was their grandmother's and that it's really old. Wink says there's nothing wrong with that, for heaven's sake. It's the American Way, by gosh. Wink can be pretty sarcastic about a lot of things. That's one reason I like him so much. He seems to be able to see through a lot of the hypocrisy and false pretenses that are in the world today.

This is one of the slowest lines I've ever seen. Three scroungy women are at the check-out counter buying a really monstrous assortment of junk and trash. There's a mile-high pile of completely unidentifiable items of clothing, rusty old baking pans and other nondescript kitchen utensils, a greasy popcorn popper, a plastic dishpan all bent out of shape, and the coup de grace — a two-foot-long plaster banjo painted purple with red polka dots.

The clerk patiently bags it all, five brown bags full,

then reaches over the counter and plunks the bags down into the shopping cart. The plaster banjo won't fit in a bag, so it's wrapped in torn newspapers.

In a minute it's obvious that something is very wrong. Then I hear that those three lowlifes want to pay with an out-of-town check.

The clerk is upset. She brushes a strand of hair off her forehead and points to a large sign hanging over the cash register: NO OUT-OF-TOWN CHECKS ACCEPTED, it says in two languages. NO EXCEPCIONS.

The clerk says something about having to get the manager, but she doesn't think he will approve the check.

The people ahead of me all sigh and shift their weight around while the clerk motions wearily for the ladies to pass the brown paper bags and the banjo back over the counter to her, where they may safely remain until the thing with the check is settled.

A heavyset black lady behind me stops talking to her friend and looks again to see what's taking so long.

"Hey now, will ya look-it dat!" she says slowly, genuinely amazed. "Now dey's givin' all deir ol' shit back."

I look at the black lady and laugh, and she smiles at me, and then she laughs, too. We laugh and laugh until the tears run down our faces.

I buy the books and start for home. I decide I'll try to put my troubles aside for now. Jamie will be coming home from school. Maybe I can cry on his shoulder.

4

My grandma Noddy is really like a second mother to me. Ever since I was in kindergarten, one of my greatest joys was bringing my little papers home to her and standing at her side in the kitchen while she looked them over carefully and lavishly praised my good work, pointing out a particularly neat line of lettering or laughing over a funny drawing. Later, when I was older, she would read my one-page themes and tell me that it was apparent that writing just seemed to "run in our family."

Grandma Noddy herself is writing a novel. She's been working on it for twenty-seven years. It all began when she enrolled in an adult night school class called Short Story Writing for Money, Fame, Publication and Personal Amusement. Toward the end of the course, the teacher read her little story out loud to the others and pronounced it "charming," and Grandma Noddy was hooked. After the course was over, she just kept adding and revising and adding and revising, and now there are more than six hundred pages of additions and revisions, and she's not finished yet.

The plot is pretty straightforward. It's about a bunch of Italian housewives in New Jersey who band together to form an organization dedicated to saving Venice. The heroine of the book is named Maria DiSalvo. Maria and the other housewives raise the sum of five billion dollars by making and selling little pizzas in obscene shapes, fast frozen and individually wrapped. The major conflict surfaces in Chapter Two, when some of the more narrow-minded ladies in the club start objecting to the pizzas on the grounds of common decency and threaten to undermine the whole project. They suggest pizzas in alternate shapes, like cute little machine guns or boots like the map of Italy. By Chapter Twelve, though, it's obvious that Maria's side will win out. Owing to the extremely warped sense of humor of the American public, the dirty pizzas are an overnight success, and one is even pictured on the cover of *Newsweek*. By Chapter Fifteen, the ladies are selling franchises worldwide, T-shirts, and little toy MAKE YOUR OWN OBSCENE PIZZAS IN THE PRIVACY OF YOUR OWN HOME kits (for adults only).

By the end of the novel, all the difficulties have been surmounted, of course, and this dauntless little band of Italian housewives is able to present the city of Venice with a huge check with which to start a reclamation project rolling. My grandma is even thinking that maybe they'll have enough money left over to save the Leaning Tower of Pisa as well. But she hasn't come to the actual writing of that part yet. She just told me about the ending.

Somewhere along the line, Grandma Noddy decided that since she was a one-book author (unlike Wink, who "spews them out like watermelon seeds"), she wanted to inculcate (her word) within her masterpiece a really universal and compelling theme. She decided that she didn't want *her* book to be just another fly-by-night novel about Italian housewives saving Venice by making suggestive pizzas; she wanted *her* book to live forever. So she stuck in her theme, and it was this: "Dare to dream the impossible dream." Uncle Wink just started clucking his tongue and shaking his head at this turn of events. He said she really blew it; she had a good story going there until she started to mess around with it by sticking in a theme. He said he knew what he was talking about; he had sold over one hundred romantic novels, and there wasn't a theme or an ounce of thought in any one of them, and then he threw his head back and laughed uproariously.

As for me, I hadn't even the foggiest notion of where Venice was, let alone that it needed to be saved. Actually, in those days I used to get it confused with Vienna. I remember telling Jamie that I never could get it straight which one was the city and which was the country — that's how mixed up I was.

My grandma cleared it all up for me, though. She got out a map of Europe one day when I was still in elementary school and showed me where Venice is, way up there in the right-hand corner of Italy. Then she went to her cedar chest in the bedroom and got out this old book of photographs of Venice that my grandfather had given her when they were married. She showed me the canals and gondolas and *pontes*. *Pontes* are bridges. The book said there are more than 450 *pontes* in the city of Venice and not one automobile. To someone from Los Angeles, it sounded like a very lovely place, the way she described it.

The only trouble is, it's sinking. The whole city is slowly sinking into the blue Adriatic Sea. Grandma Noddy always gets tears in her eyes when she talks about Venice sinking away into oblivion.

After she put the map away that day, she came up to me and took my hand. "Robin," she said, leaning toward me, "you know, I've never told this to anyone, except my boys, of course, but Muncie promised me on the day we were married that he would take me there, to Venice, on the fiftieth anniversary of our wedding."

I didn't know if the tears in her eyes then were for Venice or for the memory of that promise made so long ago.

I see my grandfather sitting on his porch as I turn the corner onto our street. I'm loaded down with the stuff from school, plus the big bag of books from the Goodwill, so I'm glad I'm almost home.

My grandparents' house is next door to ours, and there are actually two houses on their lot, but you can only see the front one from the street. I love looking at our two houses: theirs like a fairy cottage, painted green with white shutters, and ours like an older sister, larger, more imposing, cream-colored, and homey. Just seeing them now, knowing that I don't have to go back to school until the third of January, makes me sigh with relief.

I go up the shady walk leading to my grandfather's porch. The steppingstones are covered with moss. I wonder how my grandfather is feeling today.

Alzheimer's. Such an ugly word. At first he joked about it darkly. But I could tell he wasn't really joking; I saw the look in his eyes.

"Probably Alzheimer's," he'd say with a grimace when he couldn't remember where he'd left his pipe.

"Now, what was I saying . . ." he'd begin. "I can't seem to remember what we were talking about. It's that goddamn Alzheimer's."

And Muncie knew what he was talking about. He had been a general practitioner for thirty-two years and had seen plenty of Alzheimer's at first hand.

Not too long after the early symptoms first appeared, he and Grandma Noddy made an appointment to see his old partner, Dr. Morris. Although an autopsy is needed to diagnose Alzheimer's correctly, Dr. Morris's impressions were not good. My grandfather was seventy-one years old last month. Two weeks after Christmas, on January 6, he and Grandma Noddy will celebrate their fiftieth wedding anniversary. Their Venice year.

The night after they had seen Dr. Morris, Muncie took my grandma's hand and looked into her eyes. "I will take

45

you to Venice on our anniversary," he said in front of us all. "That much I promise you."

I set the bag from the Goodwill down on the wide porch railing and take off my backpack. One of my gym shoes falls out.

"You dropped your watch," my grandfather says. It's an old joke between us.

I laugh. "Hi, Muncie. How you doing?" I sit down on the swing beside him.

He pats my hand. "Remember that time you really did drop your watch? You were just a little tyke."

"I was in the sixth grade. It was a new watch, too. My first digital."

My grandfather turns to look at me. "What?" he asks, puzzled.

"My watch. It was a digital."

"Oh." He nods. But I'm not sure he understands. I decide to let it go.

Neither one of us speaks. I sneak a look at him. He's pursing and unpursing his lips. I have the feeling that he's trying to make me think that he's thinking about something, that he's philosophizing just like he used to do, and that he's on the verge of saying something wonderful.

I push on the wooden porch floor with my feet, making the swing go a little higher. It starts to squeak.

"A mouse somewhere," my grandfather says, extremely pleased with himself.

The screen door opens. "I thought I heard some conversation out here," Grandma Noddy says.

I smile at her. "How's the book and old Maria DiSalvo?" I ask. Maria and the other women in the book are practically part of our family now. Heck, they've been around longer than I have.

Uncle Wink's silver Honda pulls into the driveway before my grandma can answer. Since his divorce, Wink lives in the little house in back. His ex-wife has the big place in Palos Verdes. My mother told me her boyfriend — who happens to be her hairdresser — lives there with her now. It seemed odd to refer to a forty-year-old man as a boyfriend. Wink's got plenty of money, of course, and could live anyplace he wanted. I guess he likes it out back because it's near us and everything. Wink would have made a great father. He treats Jamie and Naomi and me kind of like substitute kids, since he and his ex-wife never had any of their own.

"Come on inside, Robin," my grandma says now. "I want to talk about Christmas."

We go inside and I sit down at the kitchen table. Grandma Noddy gets a couple of lemons out of a bag and starts to squeeze them in the juicer. "I'm sick and tired of stuffing turkeys and baking pies," she says.

I'm surprised, but I don't say anything.

"And that mother of yours," she continues, "well, she's no help at all. Especially now, since she's all tied up with that Nachos and Stinky case, or whatever those mutts' names are."

"Macho and Chinky."

"Whatever."

"Listen," I suggest, "I'll help you. I can go to the store and help with the pies and stuff. Just make a list."

She shakes her head. "No. I don't want to do that this year. It's time for a change. This year I want to do something different."

I shrug. "Okay. What?"

"Just a minute, honey," she says. She takes a tall glass of lemonade out to my grandfather. Then she comes back and fixes a glass for me. She sits down across from me at the table and leans her chin on her hand. I notice her eyes are glazing over the way they do whenever she's on the verge of something weird. The last time I saw her look like that was when she decided she wanted to parachute jump to celebrate her sixty-fifth birthday. She did it, too.

"So," I ask, "what's your idea?"

"TV dinners," she says.

"Oh, brother."

"But we'll have a drawing." She laughs an evil laugh. "One person gets left out. No dinner at all."

"Great." I'm being sarcastic. "That's really great, Grandma."

"Look at it this way, Robin," she says. "I've been fixing holiday dinners for forty years and I'm sick of it." She smiles a bit apologetically. "Okay, wait a second. How's this? We'll also have one steak."

I'm beginning to see the possibilities. "How about having the person who gets left out of the TV dinners, well, he has to fix the steak for the — "

"Perfect!" she breaks in. "Now we're off and running. Let's send someone over to the neighbor's. How about that?" She picks up the phone and pushes a number. She has instant dial.

"Marlene?" she says. Marlene's her pal across the street. "What time are you having Christmas dinner this year?" Pause. "Just the kids coming over?" Another pause. "Got room for one more?" Grandma Noddy gives me a victory signal. "No, not me," she says into the phone. Then she adds, "At least I don't think it'll be me. We're having a drawing." She winks at me. "Yes. Like a raffle. Loser goes to your place." She laughs loudly. "Yeah. That's what I say. Okay, then, Marlene. Thanks. Talk to you later."

She hangs up the phone and reaches for a piece of notepaper. "Let's see. So what do we have so far?"

"Well, let's have two TV dinners," I suggest. "Uh, one meat loaf and one, uh, the Mexican combo."

Grandma Noddy is making a list. "Okay. First person gets a meat loaf TV dinner. Person two, a Mexican combo. Third one gets to barbecue a steak for person number four." She's really speed-writing now. "And one person goes over to Marlene's."

"Right."

We look at each other, temporarily stymied.

"How about the Burger King?" I suggest. "Someone could go there."

"Sure," she agrees. "To eat there or take out?"

"Eat there. It might be kind of different on Christmas Day."

"And how about this, as an interesting adjunct? The Burger King person will be instructed to bring back here the first person he sees that he knows. He has to invite that person back here for dessert."

"Dessert? Who's going to make it? This is your Christmas off, remember?"

"We'll have ice cream and cookies."

"Oh, no," I say. "Much too common. That's much too common for such a memorable Christmas dinner as this one."

"Oreo soup, then," she says without hesitation. "A nice bowl of milk with Oreos in it. Marlene told me her grandkids love to do that."

"Grandma," I say, not without admiration, "you're really nuts."

"Thank you, my dear." She's working on the list again. "Let's send two people out for a really nice dinner. Something fancy. That'll make for an interesting contrast, don'tcha know."

"Well, okay," I agree. "But we should do something to make them feel a *little* uncomfortable."

"Their shoes won't match."

"What?"

"We'll send them to Chasen's or somewhere, but their shoes won't match. One dress shoe and one jogging shoe, something like that. It's kind of silly, I know, but still . . ."

She counts up the list. "Okay, that leaves just one more person to account for if your grandmother Boyd is coming, which, I suppose, she is."

"I guess she is. I haven't heard otherwise."

"Hmm," Grandma Noddy is murmuring. "That might pose a bit of a problem. You know your grandmother Boyd. If she decided not to cooperate, she could foul up everything." She bites the end of the pencil. "Maybe we could sort of warn her first. Get her to agree to go along with, uh, our plans."

"Maybe so." I lower my voice. "And what about, what about Muncie? If he — I mean, he won't be able to . . ."

My grandma draws a quick breath. "Yes. Well, we'll see what we can do about that."

I'm sorry I brought it up. "Listen," I say brightly, trying to recapture our jovial mood, "shall I call Grandmother Boyd? I could sound her out, tell her that we're doing something a little different this year. Give her a chance to back out."

She makes a be-my-guest gesture, so I pick up the phone and dial my grandmother Boyd in Pasadena. We have a very strange relationship. I've always felt that she really doesn't like me very much. She tries to hide it, though, by being super nice to me at times. I think I know the reason for her not liking me; it's because I remind her of Tracy.

She doesn't answer right away, so I let the phone ring longer. She's probably out poking around in her roses, finding fault with the gardener. She has a huge rose

51

garden out in her back yard. It looks like a park out there. She's got winding cement paths and a pretty little gazebo that she had built the year before I was born. There's a fish pond, too, with goldfish. She feeds the fish and prunes the roses, but a gardener does all the rest.

I don't know what my grandmother Boyd does when she answers the phone, but it takes about an hour between the time she picks up the receiver until she finally says in that refined way of hers, "Hell-o?"

"Hello, Grandmother," I say. "This is Robin. How are your feet?"

That always throws her.

Grandmother Boyd couldn't care less about Venice; she spends most of her time worrying about her feet. For several years now she's been laboring under the delusion that her left foot is shrinking. She keeps kicking off her "house shoes" (Grandmother Boyd is the only person I know who calls slippers "house shoes") and holding up her feet for purposes of comparison. And it's not a pretty sight, believe me. She used to be a ballet teacher in the olden days, and her feet are a royal mess.

"Just look at that!" she'll say. "You can't tell *me* that foot is not shrinking."

I've found that the best way to handle the situation is to agree with her, but not too strongly. If you disagree, she'll only argue about it more and get out the tape measure and a marking pen and finally force you to agree. On the other hand, if you agree too strongly, she practically gets hysterical. I made that mistake once. So you just stay somewhere safely in the middle and say something like, "Well, I don't know. Maybe it might be just a *teeny bit* smaller, but I don't think so."

Grandmother Boyd worries a lot about beards and mustaches, too. On men, of course. For some unfathomable reason, she looks upon every blade of male facial hair as a personal affront. Never mind if he's a swindler or a cheat, a cat burglar or an ax murderer, is he *clean-shaven?* — that's the question.

Most of all, though, Grandmother Boyd is known for her remarkable comment on Lake Tahoe. Muncie rented a big Dodge van when he retired from medicine and took us all on a vacation up there to see it. There were my parents, we three kids, Uncle Wink and his wife (this was a long time ago, before the divorce) and both of my grandmothers.

We had to talk my grandmother Boyd into going. She usually doesn't like new things, like getting into vans and traveling to lakes. We live near Long Beach, and by the time we got to her place in Pasadena to pick her up, the air conditioner in the van had stopped working. So we opened all the windows. Jamie and Naomi and I loved the long drive with the wind blowing our hair. Jamie and I showed Naomi how to make that up-and-down gesture with her fist, getting truck drivers to wave and blow their big diesel horns. That nearly drove Grandmother Boyd crazy.

We finally got to Lake Tahoe just at sunset and stumbled out of the van, mesmerized by the sight of that beautiful lake, with the tall pines reflected in the water, sparkling gold and orange and blue.

"Well, Mom," my mother said finally to Grandmother Boyd, "now aren't you glad you came? Isn't that about the most gorgeous sight you ever saw?"

Grandmother Boyd surveyed the scene for about two seconds over the top of her bifocals. "Ehh," she said with a dismissing wave of her hand. "Just trees, and water."

Muncie looked over at me and crossed his eyes like a child. Then we both turned away, hiding our smiles, joined forever in a lovely and enduring conspiracy.

"Is that you, Robin?" Grandmother Boyd says in her slightly haughty way. "And how is Robin today?"

"Just fine, Grandmother. I hope I didn't catch you in the middle of something."

"Oh, no, nothing urgent," she says, but her tone of voice contradicts her words. "I was out inspecting the roses. They're just covered with aphids, you know. I've told Manuel about that time and time again, but he just doesn't seem to pay any mind."

"Oh, that's too bad," I say. "But Grandmother, I'm really calling about Christmas." I tell her we're doing something a little different this year. I tell her it's going to be a "surprise," but we really need her cooperation.

"You know I don't like surprises, my dear," she scolds gently. But I've piqued her interest. I decide there may be some life in the old girl yet.

She finally says she'll come. "But I have no transportation," she reminds me in a slight whine, as if I have forgotten that she quit driving years ago.

I tell her we'll have Jamie pick her up around one in the afternoon on Christmas Day.

"I'll be ready," she promises. "Oh, Robin?" she asks. "Are you still there?"

"Yes. I'm here."

"Well, I have *terrible* news, something really *dreadful*. Is your mother there?"

"No. She's still at work."

"Oh. I see."

"But what's wrong? Can't you tell me?"

"Well, I suppose so. It's about Dr. Arbuckle." Dr. Arbuckle is her podiatrist. She's been going to him for years. She practically worships the ground he walks on.

I prepare myself for the worst. Has her podiatrist suddenly dropped dead? Has he been arrested for smuggling dope?

"Dr. Arbuckle is . . . is . . . Well, I couldn't believe it, Robin, but he is *growing a beard!*"

"Oh, horrors," I whisper, holding the receiver away from my mouth and making a face at Grandma Noddy.

"What was that? I didn't hear you."

"I said that's too bad, Grandmother. Maybe he'll come to his senses soon and shave it off."

"Well, I certainly hope so!"

"Yes. I hope so, too. Well, we'll see you on Christmas, then, Grandmother."

"Yes. On Christmas."

I hang up the phone and look at Grandma Noddy. "Her podiatrist is growing a beard."

"Oh, my God." She laughs. "It's the end of the world, for sure."

I finish my lemonade, and as I put the glass in the sink I happen to glance out the window and glimpse my grandfather sitting on the porch. He is staring out into space, his once keen mind now filled with phantoms, making little mysteries out of the commonplace.

The large calendar hanging beside the stove catches my eye. It shows three months at a time, and the sixth of January, my grandparents' fiftieth wedding anniversary, is circled in red.

"Are you really going?" I ask quietly. "Are you really going to Venice after all?"

Grandma Noddy gets up and squeezes my hand. "Yes," she whispers, "we're really going. Wink is making all the arrangements and has agreed to come with us. I couldn't possibly manage alone. It's not the way we planned," she says, her lips trembling, "but we're going."

At first I can't say anything, so I just hug her and pat her shoulder. I find my voice after a few seconds. "Well, good-bye, Grandma. I'll see you later, okay?"

I stop by the swing on the front porch and gather up my things. Then I kiss my grandfather lightly on the cheek. "Good-bye, Muncie," I say. "I'm going home now."

He looks at me and nods, but he's been dozing and his eyes are cloudy.

5

In the living room of our house, Naomi is lying on the rug and watching TV. She is waiting for her favorite program, and in the meantime she's watching some old tapes of *The Electric Company* that Uncle Wink recorded a long time ago. "Love of Chair," the soap opera parody, is on. "And what about Naomi?" a concerned male voice says as the camera slowly backs away from the chair and the music rises to a crescendo. She loves that part the best.

Naomi is eating taco chips and getting crumbs all over the place. "And what about Naomi?" I say, imitating the male voice. "Well, Naomi is getting the rug all messed up. *That's* what about Naomi."

She looks at me. "Oh, shut up, Robin," she says pleasantly. "You want to go skateboarding?"

Naomi and I are the last skateboarders on earth. We've

been working on a routine for years and almost have it perfected and ready to take on the road.

"No. No thanks. Not now, okay?" I say.

She shrugs. "Okay. Oh, Mom called. She'll be extra late. She said she'll stop at the Colonel's on the way home if we want to wait."

"Okay."

Naomi stuffs another taco chip into her mouth, spraying the crumbs all the way to the couch. "Mom says Dad's stuck in the snack bar tonight and won't be home for dinner. Louise didn't show up again and he's going to fire her."

"Oh. Where's Jamie? Did he get home yet?"

"I don't know. Is he supposed to come home tonight?"

"Well, I thought he was."

I go to my room and shut the door. I dump my stuff on the bed and *Little Women* slips out of the Goodwill bag. I thumb through it a minute, looking at some of the colored plates, and set it aside. Then I take the blue envelope from Jennifer out of *The Scarlet Letter* and lie down on my bed. I look at her distinctive handwriting on the blue envelope and wonder when we really started to drift apart. I tear open the envelope and start to read:

> *Dear Robin:*
>   *I'm writing this in typing class and I don't have much time. I'm sorry I walked away from you in gym like that. I want to tell you this because I really do like you more than April M. but I really shouldn't be writing this at all so please BURN*

IT! I'm not being dramatic. I want you to BURN IT. Anyway, I saw Bill before fifth period for a minute and he told me he was going to pretend to come on strong to A.M. but he says he still likes you better and is only trying to make you jealous. Honest, he really said that. Those were his exact words. (I don't know why, but lately he's starting to confide in me.) Anyway, I think I've talked him into giving you another chance and you'd better take it if you're smart. So here's the plan: He says he will give you a ride (and take you home!!!) to my T-shirt party that I'm having sometime after Christmas. I'm going to try to have it on Friday night but I don't know for sure yet it depends when we get back from skiing (we're leaving right after school today and having Christmas at Big Bear) and whether or not my sister has her wisdom tooth out that day or not. Bill told me he's going to ask you next week — or maybe even today if he has the chance — so please please come with him Robin because I happen to know he's going to run for King of Hearts (and you know he'll get it if he runs) and that means he'll let everybody know he wants YOU for queen and A.M. will be OUT and you will fool her and be Queen of Hearts yourself!! Just think!!! Have a nice Xmas and I'LL SEE YOU AT MY PARTY I hope I hope.

P.S. Don't forget to wear a dirty T-shirt if you have one. If you don't have one, try to get one. I got a really great one at a sidewalk sale on Wilshire. You won't believe it, it's so obscene.

And don't forget to BURN THIS RIGHT NOW.

*P.P.S. I'm putting this in your locker because I
don't want to give it to you in drama and make
April wonder why I'm passing notes to you.*

I don't burn the letter. When my parents gave me the
responsibility of watching over Naomi after school, one
of the things they drilled into me was NO FIRES AND NO
MATCHES. Instead, I tear it up into little pieces and flush
it down the toilet. Then I go back to my bed and open
Little Women.

*"Christmas won't be Christmas without any presents,"
grumbled Jo, lying on the rug . . ."*

One of the first assignments in my public speaking class
last year was to give a two-minute extemporaneous talk
on the subject of "my favorite novel." Half the kids didn't
even have a favorite novel, so the teacher expanded the
topic to include "my favorite TV show." But I didn't have
any trouble at all. Louisa May Alcott's *Little Women* is,
without question, my all-time favorite book, and that
makes me think there must be something wrong with me.
There's not a dirty word or action in it, and with its old-
fashioned pleasures and outdated homilies, it's about as
far removed from my real world as a flight to outer space.
So why do I love that book so much?

Oh, Beth, please don't go to the Hummels' this time.
The baby will die, and you will catch the fever. Amy,
you're such a selfish little brat. Are you ever going to
change? And Meg, you blush so prettily when you tell

about your castles in the air. That young Mr. Brooke is just perfect for you. But Jo! Oh my Jo, this time — oh, this time please don't send your Teddy away! He's so handsome and clever and full of fun, and he loves you so. Why, oh why can't you love him, too? *It would be a lie to say I do when I don't*, you say. And he answers, *Really, truly, dear?* And my heart just breaks in two.

My face is wet with tears and I lose my place and the book slips from my hands. I shut my eyes and drift into a kind of fitful, dreamy sleep. Jo March has cut her hair and put on a pair of designer jeans and clogs. She has leaped into the twentieth century, and she is me. She is trying on T-shirts for a party. She tries them all, one after another. She can't quite make out the words printed on them, but she knows they're not right for her.

"Robin? *Rob-in!*" There's a loud knocking at my door and Naomi is calling. "It's time for dinner! Mom's home with the chicken. Come *on!*"

There's just the three of us for dinner again tonight. Dad is still at work, and Jamie has called to say he's flying to Salt Lake City with his roommate, but he'll surely be home by Christmas. I'm surprised at the depth of my disappointment; I had really counted on seeing and talking with him.

Uncle Wink drops over after dinner, as is his habit since the divorce. This time he has a quart of strawberry Frusen Glädjé and his clipboard under his arm. He scribbles down his romances on white paper clipped to his clipboard, then types them up on his word processor.

One time he wrote a whole book in three days. It's called *My Angel Fled Away Unawares*, and is about a beautiful, flaxen-haired insurance processor named Eudoxia Jinx. Unexpectedly finding herself an heiress of a large aardvark farm in Tanzania, she is pursued halfway across the African continent by the dashing Flint Manley, a shoe salesman she met on an afternoon shopping excursion in a remote village somewhere in Nigeria. The climax comes when Flint rescues her just in the nick of time from a herd of stampeding aardvarks. What a final scene that is, as he snatches her right up on his elephant and gives her a mighty kiss she's not likely to soon forget while the aardvarks stand around gawking in amazement.

But tonight Wink's paper is clean and white, indicating that a new book is about to emerge from his ever-fertile brain.

I fetch four ice cream dishes and scoop out the Frusen Glädjé, saving the last spoonfuls stuck to the bottom of the carton for myself.

After we eat our ice cream, Naomi goes in and turns on the TV, and my mom calls out to her, as usual, "Naomi! Shut off that set, please, and go do your homework!"

Naomi comes back to the kitchen with an incredulous look on her face. "Mom," she says, exasperated, "it's *Christmas vacation!*"

"Oh," Mom says, chagrined. "I'm sorry. I guess I forgot."

Now Mom goes in to watch TV with Naomi, and Wink and I stay in the kitchen.

"Well, Robin," Wink says, "I have new worlds to conquer."

"Yeah? What?"

"My publisher wants me to do a teen romance for a new series they're putting out called Luv'n Stuff Books. But I've never done a teen book before, and I'm afraid I've lost touch with the cupcake crowd. I need some help, Robin, and I think you're the person who can give it to me."

"Really? What can I do?"

"Mostly, you can clue me in about what's going on these days with people your age. Listen, I've got it! We'll pretend you're the heroine. I'll just do a little embellishing here and there."

"Like lengthen my hair and turn it to flaxen," I tease, "and make me beautiful?"

Wink is not the type to fall into that kind of a trap. He just makes a face at me and takes his pen out of his shirt pocket and removes the top.

"Okay," he starts, "so what's the biggest thing that can happen to a high school girl nowadays?" He holds up his hand, stopping me from answering right away. "I mean, to an ordinary kid, a popular kid, not some gloomy outsider."

"Most kids are outsiders, Wink," I say softly. "The so-called in crowd is pretty select, you know. Most kids are on the outside, wishing they were in."

He nods. "Touché. But this is fiction. Escape fiction at that. *Everybody's* in. So what's the big thing? Homecoming Queen? Cheerleader?"

I'm starting to feel uncomfortable. "I guess Queen of Hearts is pretty desirable," I say at last, "at least at my school. She presides over the biggest dance of the year and has a whole page in the yearbook."

"Queen of Hearts it is, then. That's her goal." He winks at me. "Want to bet she makes it? Now, what about her boyfriend? Tall, dark and handsome still the watchwords?"

Since Bill is the closest I've ever come to having a boyfriend, I naturally think of him. "Oh, blonds are fine," I say, "as long as they have a tan, of course. Tans are very important."

"Gotcha."

"Some of them have cute, lopsided smiles," I say, "and they're big on sports."

Wink is taking all this down. "Baseball, soccer, football?"

"You can't lose with football. Football's probably the best."

"Some things never change," Wink murmurs. "What else?"

I suck on my spoon, holding it upside down in my mouth. Then I remove it, examine it closely, and start to fantasize. "Well, a real boyfriend is also someone you can *talk* to. You're not afraid to tell him how you really feel and what you really think. You can tell him your fears and your hopes. And he tells you his." I look down at my fingernails and start picking at the cuticles. Wink is still writing. He must be adding some thoughts of his own. He pauses now, and I decide to give it my all. "And with a real boyfriend," I say quietly, "you don't feel torn all the time, and you don't have to think that sex is something funny and gross, but you really know that it's beautiful, and private, and . . . and sacred." I'm practically whispering now, and I look up to see old Wink watching me with such understanding and compassion, it almost makes me feel like crying.

Wink nods his head and puts his pen away. "I think that's fine," he says. "I think that gives me plenty to work on."

We sit there at the table and talk of other things, and pretty soon my dad comes home and he and Wink have a cup of coffee together and "shoot the breeze," as Wink says. It's fun watching them together. They're like a couple of kids, friends and pals forever.

I leave them and go to my room. Soon I'm back in that bittersweet land with Meg and Jo and Amy and Beth. Another Christmas has rolled around, and they each have a special gift to treasure: a book for Jo, a dress for Meg, a picture for Amy, and some grapes for sick little Beth. And, suddenly, the greatest gift of all — their beloved father appears, home safely from the war.

6

It's the third day of Christmas vacation and I sleep late again. Naomi and I go out skateboarding, and in the afternoon I treat her to a movie. Life is easygoing and pleasant, and I find myself wishing that I never have to see old Southside High again.

In the evening Wink comes over and we all watch a little TV, and then Wink and I go into the kitchen and talk about the novel. Although I myself have dark hair and am on the skinny side, our heroine (just as I expected) is a "beautiful, flaxen-haired teenager whose body has not yet blossomed into its full, promised perfection." Wow. Wink decides to have the story start during her Christmas vacation, when she will meet someone new and exciting, a tall and handsome suntanned god of a boy who grins a lot with his lopsided grin and has loads of blond hair on his muscular arms. We finally decide on our heroine's name: it is Lark Greenwillow.

When we get tired of planning the novel, Wink suggests we put it away and play something he calls the People Game. He says that he and a newspaper buddy made it up back in the old days when they were cub reporters together and would hang out at the bar and grill across the street from the paper.

"It's kind of hard to explain exactly how to play it," Wink says, "since we didn't really make it up. We just kind of fell into it. So why don't you just listen, and I'll try to demonstrate." He leans back in his chair and takes a deep breath. Pretty soon he says, "Well, I ran into old Jim Hocking today." He pauses then to explain. "That's how you start, see? Your opening sentence is like an introduction."

He starts off again. "Anyway, I ran into old Jim Hocking today. He used to be a cameraman for Charlie Chaplin, and he still has some of his fingernail clippings that he saved and wrapped up in a paper napkin back in the twenties."

"Gee," I say. "Is that really true?"

"Sure is. Has to be. That's the game. It has to be true. Here's another one, a short one, a kind of variation." He smoothes back what's left of his hair. "I got my hair cut yesterday. My barber lives in a tree house."

"I laugh. "Come on, Wink."

"No," he protests. "It's true. He really does. He built it himself. It was written up in the real estate section several months ago. But anyway, do you get the idea? You simply describe people in a way that makes them stand out from everybody else. The more unusual, the better. Go on now, you try it. It's good practice for our novel."

"Uh." I falter after a minute. "I can't think of anything."

"Oh, sure you can. Think about your friends. What's unusual about them?"

My mind's a blank. "I guess you'd better get a new assistant, Wink. I just can't think of anything. None of my friends is outstanding in any way."

"Hmm. That's hard to believe. How about your teachers, or someone you know at — "

"Hold it," I say suddenly. "I think I've got one. It's about our vice-principal, Mr. Bussone."

"Shoot," says Wink.

"The vice-principal at school is named Mr. Bussone."

"Yeeesss?" Wink says, looking very attentive and smiling slightly. "What about him?"

I clear my throat. "Mr. Bussone, our, uh, *beloved* vice-principal, picks garden snails off this hedge at school and eats them whole, shell and all."

"Jesus!" Wink laughs. "Does he still do that? He used to do that when I knew him back at Pasadena JC. He used to freak us all out, eating those damn snails like that."

"Yeah. Isn't it sickening? But, hey, I thought you graduated from USC?"

"Yes. Well, I graduated from USC, but I spent my

68

first two years at the junior college. See, uh, I goofed off a little in high school, and then I spent that time bumming around Europe, and . . ."

"Oh, I get it. You had to make up some credits."

Uncle Wink is looking off into space. "I saved his life once, you know," he says.

"Whose?"

"Old Buzzy. Your Mr. Bussone."

"You're kidding! How'd you do that?"

Wink leans forward in his chair and pulls out his wallet from his back pocket. He starts taking out credit cards and other papers, lining them all up on the table. While he's doing this he says, "It was an auto accident. Some fool ran a light on Colorado Boulevard and plowed right into us. Buzz was driving. He used to drive this green Morris sedan in those days. There were four of us in the car. A guy named Lenny Wilson and his brother were in the back seat. Buzz was quite a musician, you know. He and Lenny Wilson and Lenny's brother had this little trio. They used to do a lot of old Ted Lewis stuff. Well, anyway, when this turkey hit us it was quite a jolt, to put it mildly. The back door flew open and Lenny and his brother got out okay, but old Buzz was knocked cold." Wink touches his head. "Got a nasty cut on his forehead, too. Well, I just opened my door and yanked him out. Hell, I did it without even thinking. A second later, the whole car went up in flames."

Now he takes out a yellowed piece of paper from the innards of his wallet. "Ah, here it is," he says. "I thought I still had it."

Very carefully he unfolds the paper and reads it over to himself slowly, with a kind of faraway look in his eyes. Then he hands it to me. It's really faded and torn on the folds, but I can read it okay.

> To Wink, without whom I would be fried to a crisp:
> This is to certify that "I owe you one, pal." Redeem this note for anything (and that means ANYTHING) that I can do for you now or anytime in the future. There is no expiration date on this offer, and I will not be truly at peace until it is redeemed.
>
> > With undying gratitude,
> > James P. "Buzz" Bussone, Jr.

I hand the note back to Wink. "That's really something," I say. "But nobody calls him Buzz. Everybody at school hates his guts, and we all call him 'The Buzzard.' "

The phone on the kitchen counter rings and I pick it up. It's my dad.

"Oh," he says, "Robin. Just the person I wanted to talk to. Listen, I'm in a terrible bind. Louise didn't show up for work again, and we're having a break in twenty-five minutes."

"Okay," I say. I really don't mind helping in the snack bar. All you do is fix cold drinks and hand out popcorn. "But I thought you were going to fire Louise."

"I was. But she sweet-talked her way out of it. Listen, is Wink there? Can he give you a ride over?"

"Dad needs some help for the break," I say to Wink. "Can you take me over there?"

Wink stands up. "Sure. What's the movie? Maybe we can stay over and watch it."

"Texas Chainsaw Massacre, Part Two," I joke.

Wink smiles. "Sounds delightful. Let's go."

Mom comes home unexpectedly at around two in the afternoon on the day before Christmas and slams her briefcase down on the desk. "Now those sneaky bastards want to settle out of court," she announces. "Can you believe it?"

"Watch your language, Mom," I say. We always keep telling each other to watch our language. Then I ask, "Who? You can't mean old Macho and Chinky!"

"No. Their pinbrained owners. The whole suit was just the final salvo in some idiotic lovers' quarrel. I should have spotted it from the beginning, but the fact that Chinky has a pedigree three miles long and her pups are worth a mint blinded me to the true reason behind it all. Listen, my head's splitting. I'm going to lie down for a while."

I start dinner while she's sacked out in the den. Since it's Christmas Eve, my dad closes the theater and spends the afternoon reading and clipping movie reviews. He's really excited because one of our TV channels called and offered him a two-minute spot once a month talking about what's new at the movies. I don't like going to the movies with my dad because he always starts talking about them before we're even out of the theater. It drives me crazy because I don't want to talk about them; I only want to think about them.

I put a chicken-broccoli casserole in one oven and some frozen biscuits in the other. It's a double-recipe casserole (that means it has two cans of soup), so at the last minute Naomi runs next door to see if my grandparents and Wink want to join us. We do that quite often, but in reverse. Usually it's my grandma who invites us over to her place. That's because my mom works long hours and my dad works odd ones, and Grandma Noddy knows we're pretty disorganized over here.

The three of them come over a few minutes later, and just as we're all sitting down at the table Jamie blows in, surprising us all.

"Well look!" I exclaim. "It's Mr. March, home from the war!"

Wink is the only one who catches it. "Fetch his slippers, Jo," he says, "and go call Marmee."

I sit down beside him. The others are all noisily talking among themselves. "How did you know that?" I ask with a smile.

"Know what?"

"About Jo, and Marmee."

"Well, how do you think? I'm not a complete illiterate, you know."

"Yes, but *Little Women?* I didn't think members of the male sex ever read that book. None of the guys I know would be caught dead within ten feet of it, that's for sure."

Wink starts to tell me a little about Louisa May Alcott

and her father, then, how he was a philosopher and a teacher. I tell him I think Louisa May was a genius and I would give anything to have had a chance to meet her.

Wink starts to answer, but Naomi tells me she thinks the biscuits are burning, so I go and rescue what's left of them, which isn't much.

After dinner, Jamie and I clean up in the kitchen, just like before he went away to school. Only now it's funny, we don't argue about every little thing, like the time we spent an hour debating about who should put the pot-holder away.

I think about telling him what happened in Mr. Huntsman's class and how I've been feeling more and more lost in the crowd and uncomfortable around my friends, and about Jennifer's note and her T-shirt party and Bill and all that, but I really don't feel like opening that can of worms right now. Besides, school seems like a million miles away.

Pretty soon we finish up in the kitchen and go in and join the others. Grandma Noddy doesn't spill the beans about the unusual Christmas dinner the two of us have planned, so I keep the lid on, too.

7

After a pleasant but fairly subdued Christmas morning (except when Naomi opens the big cardboard box and pulls out her new skateboard), my parents, Naomi and I cross over the lawn to Muncie and Grandma Noddy's house. Jamie has already left to pick up Grandmother Boyd.

Next door, we find Uncle Wink sitting in the front room with the newspaper, making occasional comments about not smelling any turkey in the oven and what the hell is going on, anyway. While the others are talking, Naomi and I sneak into the kitchen and snitch handfuls of chocolate chips from Grandma Noddy's jar.

Pretty soon Jamie and Grandmother Boyd walk in the door. She's all spiffed up in an outfit I've never seen before, and she's obviously just had her hair done, since it looks all silvery, like sterling. She's telling Jamie she has some little chores she'd like him to do when he takes her back home, if he has the time. "Sure, Grandmother," Jamie says. Jamie is definitely one of the good guys. Some of my friends have older brothers, too, and I can't believe the stories they sometimes tell about what bums they are. When the kids ask me about Jamie, I try not to brag about him, though. I just say, "Oh, he's okay."

We're finally all gathered in the living room in front of the tree, and Grandma Noddy takes center stage. She's really in her element. She apologizes for not having dinner ready and says she has something better planned. Then she explains about the drawing, and I watch the reactions of my family. They're really funny. Mom sighs and looks over at Dad as if to say, "Well, she's *your* mother," and Dad grins and rubs his hands together, eager to join wholeheartedly in whatever wild and crazy scheme his mother has come up with this time. Jamie laughs nervously and looks somewhat amazed while Wink impatiently exclaims, "For Chrissake, Mom, how'd you hatch this harebrained plan?"

Naomi keeps looking around at the rest of us, waiting for a cue before taking a stand, but thoroughly confused by the varying reactions she sees. Because she was warned, Grandmother Boyd is not totally surprised. In fact, she puts on an air of nonchalance and says irritably, "Well, come on, Noddy. You've explained it long enough. Let's just have your drawing and be done with it."

The steak dinner at home is won by Wink. "Well, all *right!*" he says with a sudden change of attitude. "Nothing wrong with that." Grandma Noddy, of all people, is the one who is to cook it. "Can you beat that?" she asks good-naturedly. "I think it's called 'reaping what you sow.' "

The TV dinners are drawn by Mom and Dad. "Just like the good old days in Berkeley, isn't it, Mother?" Dad says to Mom enthusiastically. Mom looks at him as though he's absolutely insane.

Naomi is overjoyed to be picked for going across the street to Marlene's, who has a grandson about her age. "I hope he brought his skateboard," Naomi says. "I want to go over there right now! Can I? Can I, Mom?" She gets up and starts prancing around the room.

"Naomi!" Mom scolds. "You calm down now. Just settle down."

Naomi gets on her famous pout, an expression that always seems to set my mother off like a pistol.

Mom stares at her. "And get that sour expression off your face this instant, young lady." Mom looks at her even more closely now. "And have you been into your grandma's chocolate chips again?"

Naomi unconsciously wipes off her lips and shakes her head; my mother lets the subject drop.

I quietly get up and go to the bathroom, and while I'm there I wash traces of chocolate off my hands. When I go back to the front room, I notice that Muncie is looking even more confused than usual at this point, and I hear Grandma Noddy tell him quietly that she has a nice meat pie in the oven for him. Then she announces that we'd better finish the drawing.

What's left is the dinner at Chasen's for two and a lone trip to the Burger King — and Jamie, Grandmother Boyd, and me.

"The first winner of an all-expense trip to the world-famous Chasen's restaurant with mismatched shoes is . . ." Grandma Noddy draws a name. ". . . is Elsie Boyd!"

We all applaud wildly, and I'm happy to see that Naomi has stopped her pouting.

"Well, that's *very* nice," Grandmother Boyd manages to say, lightly patting a silver curl at her temple. I think it's very lucky she won the Chasen's prize, since she really enjoys expensive dinners at classy restaurants.

"What was that bit about mismatched shoes?" Jamie asks after we quiet down again.

"Oh, that." Grandma Noddy rubs her chin. "Well," she says innocently, "the lucky diners at Chasen's will just wear mismatched shoes, that's all."

Apparently, Grandmother Boyd missed hearing that the first time around. "What do you mean, Noddy?" she asks sharply. There is not much love lost between the two of them, anyway. "Why on earth would they want to do that?"

"Obviously, Elsie, they wouldn't *want* to," Grandma Noddy answers simply, "but those are the rules." Then she shrugs, as if she herself had nothing to do with it. She turns to me and says, "Oh, Robin, do you suppose you could run home and get one of your old jogging shoes for your grandmother? You look about the same size."

"Okay, as soon as the drawing is over." I'm anxious to see what I'm going to win.

Grandma Noddy nods her head and draws another name. There are only two left — mine and Jamie's. "The lucky person accompanying Elsie Boyd to Chasen's is . . . Mr. Jamie Tweedy-Boyd!"

We all clap and stomp our feet.

"And that leaves a lovely Christmas dinner alone at the Burger King for our little Robin. Now don't forget, Robin, you're to ask the first person you meet that you know back here for dessert."

I run home and get the shoe for Grandmother Boyd, and Jamie goes home, too, and comes back wearing a hiking boot on one foot and a tennis shoe on the other.

I'm really proud of Grandmother Boyd, the way she carries it off. I think she just wants to prove to Grandma Noddy that she can handle whatever foolishness is dished out. She takes Jamie's arm, and the two of them leave the room like a couple of vaudeville comedians, soft-shoeing sideways out the door.

Grandma Noddy slips me a five-dollar bill, and I leave for the Burger King as they call out, "Good luck, Robin, and Merry Christmas!"

The Burger King is only a few blocks away, over in the shopping center next to the Goodwill Store. It's a nice day for a walk. The fog has lifted, but the sky is still cloudy and gray. It may even rain, but I don't mind. The streets are almost deserted, and so far I haven't seen anyone I know. I guess the neighbors are all inside with their families.

Once I leave our block, the scenery is pretty dismal. I think about how many of the suburbs of Los Angeles have such beautiful names — like Downey, and Bellflower, and Artesia, but so many of the streets are just a mishmash of empty or rundown storefronts, apartment buildings, upholstery shops and gas stations.

There are only three customers in the Burger King: an old man sitting alone, smoking a cigarette and looking out the window with half-closed eyes, and a teenaged mother with a kid in a flimsy stroller. The kid is smashing soggy french fries with his fist and then stuffing them in his eyes, ears and nose in just about equal proportions, as far as I can tell. The mother is reading a romance and making sucking noises with her straw.

I go up and order a Whopper, fries, and a chocolate shake. After a second I add onion rings. After all, it's Christmas.

While I'm waiting for my order, I try to make out the author's name on the romance the kid's mother is reading. It's not Prudence Penrose Honeysuckle, but that's no surprise. There must be ten billion romances floating around out there.

When my order's ready, I go and sit down somewhere midway between the old man and the mother and kid. I look out the window and contemplate the asphalt. I notice that some weeds are growing right through the gray-green Tuff-Turf that lines the walk. Nature will have its way.

The kid starts whimpering and the mother tells him to shut up. Surprisingly, he does. The old man puts out his cigarette and rests his head on his folded arms. Some Christmas, I think.

I check my Casio: 2:14 57, 2:14 58, 2:14 59, 2:15 00. It seems to me that time flows on like a river, but Jamie told me that's not the way it works. He was told in his physics class that time does not flow. Time, like space, is just there.

Suddenly, without warning, I'm filled with an overwhelming sense of sadness and loss for my grandfather, who is slowly and painfully, piece by piece, being taken away from me — from all of us.

I wipe a tear from my eye and wonder what made me think of him now. And then I remember: *You dropped your watch.* What makes our brains work like that, connecting bits and pieces, odd thoughts and old songs, in spite of ourselves? Do we think about what we *want* to think about, or are those connections made in keeping with the laws of chemistry, inexorably planned? Suddenly I feel so sorry for everyone in the world, I can't stand it.

The door of the Burger King swings open and I catch my breath. Oh, my God, it's Emery Day.

He doesn't even look around. He just makes a beeline for the restroom, rubbing one eye with the back of his hand. A split second passes before I realize — good grief! —

I have to try to bring *him* back home with me.

Quickly I turn and face the windows, putting my back to the restrooms. He might not even notice me. But my conscience doesn't let me get away with that for long. I imagine the battle royal that must be taking place in my brain. Ever since Jamie told me a little bit about brains and how they work, I keep picturing what's going on up there, those neurotransmitters hopping over those synapses like crazy, lighting up (so to speak) those billions of neurons like some out-of-control computer game. The verdict comes in like a flash; I turn around in my seat. I'll leave it to fate. If he sees me, he sees me; if he doesn't, he doesn't. That's fair enough.

He sees me. He comes out of the restroom dabbing at his eye with a handkerchief and blinking like a goldfish. He does a wonderfully genuine double take and, after a slight hesitation, walks uncertainly over to where I'm sitting. He's wearing his usual plaid flannel shirt and that Levi's vest.

"Is that Robin Tweedy-Boyd?" he asks, exaggerating his hesitancy, peering at me from behind the handkerchief.

"Hi, Emery," I say as matter-of-factly as possible, all the while wondering how I'm ever going to explain my forthcoming invitation without sounding like a complete weirdo.

"Robin Tweedy-Boyd," he repeats, almost to himself. "Robin Tweedy-Boyd."

I know what's coming by the tone of his voice: some

stupid comment about my name. When they start repeating it like that, watch out. Stupid comment not far behind.

"You know," he says, putting his handkerchief in his back pocket and letting one knee drop on the seat opposite me, "I think it's really neat how some parents give their kids such cute names . . ."

I exhale rudely. "Oh, spare me . . ."

"No, I mean it. It gives them kind of a permanent icebreaker, don't you see?"

I just look at him.

"So you don't see. Well, okay. Take me, for instance. Emery Day." He grimaces. "As far as names go, zero. Right?"

"Worse than zero. Emery Day is definitely a minus."

He chooses to ignore that comment. Instead, he says, "Now, suppose my parents — well, let's suppose they'd used their imagination and named me something like, oh, Washington."

"Washington?" I say. "Why Washington?"

"Wash Day?" He sits himself all the way down in the seat now. He shakes his head and makes a funny noise with his mouth. "Wash Day," he repeats slowly. "God, with a name like that, I would really clean up. I'd probably be student body president by now." He looks away for a second and adds, almost to himself, "And would my mom love *that*."

"It takes more than a name," I say.

I take a bite of hamburger and then gather up all the

lettuce and junk that falls on my napkin and eat that, too. "Emery," I say, "why did you cry so much in the fourth grade?" Then I look at his face.

First of all, he looks surprised. Then he looks so pained, I think for a second he's going to start crying again right here and now. That look soon melts into something more like acceptance or understanding, however, and then I think he might even laugh. But he doesn't. Then there's an expression I can't figure out. It might be disappointment.

"Search me," he says finally. He turns and walks to the counter, and I hear him order a medium Coke. He comes back to where I'm sitting and swirls the ice around in his cup.

I don't know why, but I don't give up. It's something like the chickens in the chicken pen. I can't help picking on him. "But *why* did you cry all the time?"

He looks at me squarely this time. His eyes are dark blue, like the sky at sunset, but they're framed in red, as if his tears are made of blood.

"Maybe because I was so goddamn happy," he says.

His answer stuns me, not only the words, but the steadiness of his gaze and the strength of his sarcasm.

"I'm sorry," I hear myself murmur. "I — "

"What are you doing here, anyway?" he interrupts briskly. He finishes his Coke. "Isn't this Christmas? You run away from home or something?"

"Well, what about you?" I answer. I'm just not ready to hit him with an invitation to my grandma's house for

83

a nice bowl of Oreo soup. Not yet, anyway. "Isn't this Christmas for you, too?"

"Jehovah's Witnesses don't celebrate Christmas."

"Really? You're a Jehovah's Witness?" I ask, thinking, my God, what next?

"Not anymore. But my mom is."

"Your mom is, but you're not?"

"That's what I said. You have ear trouble or something, Robin?"

"Well, how come you're not?" I ask, on the defensive now. "I mean, if your mother . . ."

Emery looks past my right ear up to the circulating fan on the ceiling and sighs heavily. Then he picks up one of my french fries, holding it at one end and letting it flop over limply. "You really want to know?" he asks, biting the french fry in half.

"Of course. Why else would I ask?"

His eyes search my face for a moment, as if he's looking for a clue that might expose an ulterior motive. Apparently I pass muster, because he says, "I'm not a Jehovah's Witness for the simple reason that several years ago I did some pretty serious thinking about religion and ultimately decided it wasn't for me."

"Just like that?"

"No. Not 'just like that.' It was a long, drawn-out process. But you see, I'm condensing it for you. What happened was I finally decided that the main reason for religion is the fear of death. And I'm . . ." He pauses, watching me closely.

"Yes?"

84

"And I learned not to be afraid of death." He eats the other half of the french fry. "And I also decided about that time that there's no such thing as a so-called soul. I read a lot of Bertrand Russell, guys like that. I decided your soul, your mind" — he points to his head — "it's all right up here in your brain. When you die" — he snaps his fingers — "it dies."

I can't believe I'm sitting in the Burger King on Christmas Day talking to Emery Day about souls. "You can't prove that, though," I say, challenging him.

"Well, no. But I figure the burden of proof for the existence of the soul lies on the shoulders of the . . ." He's finally at a loss for words.

"Perpetrators?" I suggest.

"The perpetrators?" He nods. "Okay. Whoever came up with the notion of a supernatural soul, let them prove it."

"That was probably God," I say dryly.

He laughs outright in a sudden burst of merriment. "Well, as far as I know, there's never been any scientific evidence whatsoever that such a thing as a soul exists. Of course, I mean, if and when they do discover something tangible, well, then I may have to rethink the whole thing. But I really don't think there's any danger of that. I think when we're dead we're dead. Right? We decay, just like everything else. Our brains, our souls, our minds — it all decays. So what's the big deal? Why can't people face up to that?" He takes the last french fry, a small burned one, and eats it in one gulp.

"I guess it's just not a very pretty picture."

He shrugs. "Where does it say it has to be pretty? That's just the way it is. I think you have to look at things the way they are and make the best of it."

He looks at his watch. "Well, enough of this heavy stuff, Robin Tweedy-Boyd. I've got to get going." He pats his vest pockets as though he's checking to see if everything is still there.

I stand up, too, and start to gather all my trash together. "Oh, wait a minute, will you, Emery? I've got to ask you something."

"Oh, no. Don't tell me. Not *that* again."

I turn to look at him and realize he's teasing me about the crying business. God, he's so short, but his hair is not the same carrot red it used to be when he was younger. I notice it's much darker now, sort of a reddish brown, the same as his eyebrows, which are really thick and heavy over his deeply set eyes.

I guess I'm just staring at him, not knowing what to say, when he suddenly breaks into a smile. He doesn't have to say he was only kidding because I know that's what he means.

"Listen," I say, "this is kind of hard to explain, but the bottom line is that I'm supposed to invite you over to my grandparents' house for dessert this afternoon."

He cocks his head to one side as if he didn't hear me right. "What was that again?"

So I explain the whole thing, starting with my nutty grandma who was tired of cooking Christmas dinners and ending with the fact that he is, indeed, the first person I saw that I know.

He shakes his head and looks a little doubtful, as if he suspects I might be playing some kind of trick on him.

I hold up my right hand. "Sounds crazy, I know, but . . ."

"You're right. It sure does. But what the heck? Why not? I'm game. But I have to go back home first. Listen, I've got my bike. Did you walk over?"

"Yes."

"Well, come on. I'll give you a lift to my place, and then we can go over to your, uh, nutty grandma's."

"On the bike?" I ask, not sure what he means. "Both of us, on the bike? Can you . . ."

"Robin Tweedy-Boyd," he says, moving close to my ear and speaking in a low, deep voice, "I'm *very* powerful."

"Okay," I answer, slightly flustered. "If you think you can handle it."

I take my trash over to the garbage can. Emery is over at the door now, opening it for somebody. I see it's old Jake, the can man. Jake is trying to push his grocery cart inside the restaurant and is having some trouble getting it through the door. All the while, he's showing off his new T-shirt for Emery, telling him how the gang at the Burger King gave it to him for Christmas.

I'm surprised Emery is talking to Jake at all. I mean, I've seen him around for years, and maybe I'll say hi sometimes, but I never stand around and talk to him.

Right now Jake's pointing to the printing on his T-shirt. It's got JAKE THE CAN MAN in a semicircle at the top, and right in the center is a sketch of a small brown-furry animal being tossed into a garbage can. Under the can it says, "After they made me, they threw away the mole."

Jake laughs his funny, high-pitched laugh and waves his little arms around. He's a feisty little guy, only about four feet high, and next to him Emery actually looks tall. Jake walks with a limp because of his wooden leg. He's supposed to have lost his leg in the war, but that's highly doubtful unless he was a spy or something, because I'm sure they'd never take him in the regular army. He also looks odd because of his eye. He lost one eye in some kind of street scuffle several years ago and had it replaced with a fake one. He just hangs around the neighborhood, collecting cans and picking up the trash around the Burger King, pushing that grocery cart around and carrying all his junk in it. He's got an old ratty blanket in there and a change of clothes. I've even seen him all curled up in that cart, reading a paperback or playing softly on his ocarina. Some of the kids say he actually stays in the storage room here at the Burger King at night, but I'm not sure about that.

Emery laughs at something Jake says and slaps him on the back, and then the two of us go outside together. Emery stoops over to unlock his bike, and when he straightens up again something makes me say, "Hey, Emery, how tall are you, anyway?"

He looks at me, his face a blank, and he doesn't answer. He steadies the bike and motions for me to hop on the crossbar.

"I'm just asking," I say. "So, come on, how tall are you?"

Of course, I know how tall he is. He's the same height as me. I can't imagine why I'm so bitchy.

"I don't know," he says evenly. "What difference does it make? You getting on?"

I hop on the bike, my legs dangling down on one side and my body encased by Emery's arms. We set off, and I feel strangely confident as he maneuvers down the driveway and into the street as surely and steadily as if I were only as light as a feather. But all the same, I'm hoping I won't be seen by any of the kids from school.

8

If you go about three blocks south of the Burger King on Blossom Boulevard, you'll come to a little side street with no sidewalks that goes off at a kind of slant. The road doesn't have a street sign, and I don't even know the name of it, although I've lived in this neighborhood all my life. On the corner of Blossom Boulevard and this little side street is the Double A Truck Driving Training School, and next door to that, farther south, is the Stardust Trailer Court.

You wouldn't know it's a trailer court from the outside because it's surrounded by a high wooden fence and overgrown oleander bushes, and all you can see are the tall shade trees inside the fence. The entrance is flanked by the rotting remnants of two huge wagon wheels from the pioneer days leaning against the gateposts.

Emery coasts from the paved street across a bump and

into the graveled driveway of the trailer court and I bounce vigorously on the crossbar.

"Ouch!" I exclaim.

"Whoops. Sorry," Emery says, but he doesn't sound too sorry.

"I didn't know you lived here," I say as we get off the bike.

"Shows how much you know."

He leads me down a side path lined with pots of neglected geraniums, then drops the bike on a narrow strip of patchy grass and knocks loudly under the window of a small white and blue mobile home. He walks up to the door and opens it a crack. "Mom? Somebody's with me."

I hear a muffled response. Emery blocks the door with his body, and I understand we are to wait outside. After a few seconds of just standing there, Emery points to the mobile home across the path. On the door there's a huge family crest carved out of wood and brightly painted. "Some of the people here are big on tracing their family trees," he says quietly, as if confiding some embarrassing secret. "Pretty pitiful, huh? Almost like their final grasp at some kind of — "

He's interrupted by a call from inside. He peers around the door. "Okay, Mom?" Then he nods to me and we go inside.

I've never been in a mobile home before. It seems like a small house. It's quite dark inside, and my eyes take a while to adjust.

Emery's mother is sitting at a yellow Formica table with a half-worked jigsaw puzzle spread out in front of her. She's wearing a faded purple chenille housecoat, and she seems to be swimming in it, she's so skinny. I notice a pair of aluminum crutches leaning against the wall behind her. She looks at Emery with such love, I don't know whether to be impressed or disgusted.

"This is Robin, Mom. Robin, my mother."

"Hello, Mrs. Day," I say.

"It's so very nice to meet you, Robin. I've heard your name for so long . . ."

I hear Emery shuffling around behind me. "Yeah, well," he says, "it's funny, because I got something in my eye and stopped at the Burger King to wash it out, and lo and behold, there was Robin."

I'm looking around the room now, and my eyes finally come to rest on a large black and white photograph of a man who looks to be in his early thirties. The picture's in a gold frame and is hanging above a small couch. Because of the dim light, I can't exactly make out what he's wearing, but it looks like a uniform.

"That there's Emery's father," Mrs. Day says in her quiet drawl. "He was a driver for Pacific Interstate . . ." Her voice drops. ". . . until the accident."

"Oh, Mom," Emery begins, "she doesn't —"

"No," I say, turning to look at Emery, who's standing there with his hands in his pockets, staring at the floor. "No, that's all right."

Mrs. Day is still talking. Emery is watching me now, but his eyes quickly dart away from mine as she adds, "Emery was in the fourth grade when it happened, weren't you, dear?"

"Something like that." He takes two U-No's out of his vest pocket. "Here," he says, putting them on the table. "They were out of Milky Ways. Uh, listen, Mom, I'm going over to Robin's for — "

"Oh, here," Mrs. Day breaks in, reaching over by the phone and picking up an old torn envelope. "There's a message for you. Vicki called. She wants you to call her back."

"Oh," Emery groans. "Where is she? At home or at the hospital?"

"I don't know." His mother gives him the envelope. Her hands seem to be just bones and veins.

Emery glances at me, excusing himself with a gesture. He picks up the phone and dials. Then he says, "Vicki? What's up?"

I idly wonder who Vicki is.

"Can anyone else do it? I kind of have some plans for this afternoon. Did you try Delores?" He waits. "Sure. Okay. I'll come in tonight then. Yeah. Around six or so. That's okay. So long."

He hangs up the phone. "Anyway, Mom, I'm going to Robin's for a while."

"What about dinner, honey?" she asks. "I was going to fry up some pork chops."

"Just save mine, could you?" he asks. "I'll eat it when I get home from the hospital." He nudges my arm. "Let's go."

"It was very nice meeting you, Mrs. Day," I say. I notice with alarm that she is reaching for her crutches.

"Oh, no, please," I say. "Please don't get up."

93

She looks at Emery with what seems to be an expression of mild panic, almost as if she wants to keep me from leaving. She reaches out a hand to Emery and says, "Oh, wait. Here." She motions toward the tiny kitchen. "Take some banana bread. Please, Robin, take some banana bread. I just made it yesterday."

"No, Mom," Emery protests.

But she insists, so Emery steps into the kitchen and wraps a hunk of something in foil and says, not too kindly, really, "There. How's that, Mom?"

Mrs. Day smiles and nods and says she hopes to see me again real soon.

But Emery is rushing me out the door.

"Fourth grade, huh?" I say between my teeth before the door even shuts behind us. "Why didn't you *tell* me that's what happened?"

He hands me the foil-wrapped package. "Because I don't like to talk about it, and, besides, you didn't really care."

"Of course I cared," I answer, but down deep I realize he's right. I didn't really care, at least when I had asked him.

He's picking up the bike again, and I'm really upset. I think I'm upset mostly because he has seen right through me. He knows I was just picking on him. Something makes me do it again.

"Hey, Emery," I say, trying to make my voice innocent and helpful, "why do you wear that stupid vest around all the time, anyway?"

Emery has already straddled the bike. Now he crosses

his arms and slants his body way back in the seat, his weight on one foot. He stares at me, and I stare right back.

Finally he says, "Robin, I'm getting a little sick of all this stuff. What's eating you, anyway?"

I feel myself blushing. "Nothing's *eating* me. I was just wondering why you wear that — "

"Cut out all that bullshit, will you?"

I'm too shocked to answer.

"If I'm going to have to spend the rest of the afternoon with you, you can just cut out all that bullshit."

His words are calm, and his face doesn't look angry.

I hesitate. "Okay," I say finally. I get on the bike and we head out toward the street.

We stop at my house first, and Emery waits while I throw the banana bread in the freezer and change my sweater. We're walking across the lawn between my house and my grandparents' just as Jamie and Grandmother Boyd are pulling up in front.

"That's my brother, Jamie," I explain as they get out of the car, "and my other grandmother. She's from Pasadena."

"We had a very lovely time," Grandmother Boyd says, ignoring Emery completely. That's how she is. She simply ignores new people until she's formally introduced.

Emery notices the odd shoes right away, and as we follow Jamie and Grandmother Boyd through the door, he points to their feet with a quick little surreptitious gesture and looks at me questioningly. I just shrug, pretending that I don't know anything about it. He gives me a disbelieving look, and I begin to see that Emery's pretty hard to fool.

Wink is sitting in the front room reading the newspaper, but he stands up when we come in, still holding the paper at his side. I introduce Emery, but he doesn't make much of an impression. I'm not surprised at that, since he's just this short little nobody.

My mom and dad and Grandma Noddy come in from the kitchen, and Grandma Noddy tells Naomi to shut off the TV. I don't see Muncie around, so I presume he's taking a nap.

Everyone goes into the dining room, and I introduce Emery again to the others as "somebody I know from school." They're all polite, of course, but I notice my mother doesn't go out of her way to try to impress him, the way she does to Bill whenever he's around.

We all sit down and Grandma Noddy brings out the milk, some bowls, three packages of Oreo cookies, and some ice cold cans of A&W root beer. She passes the bowls around with a little smile on her face, but no explanations, and opens the packages of cookies and puts them on a plate. Then she places three or four Oreos in her bowl and fills it with milk, as if it's an everyday occurrence.

My family's so cool. They just follow her lead without even commenting. I wonder what Mrs. Madison from my drama class would say if she could be here now.

Emery's great, I must confess. He breaks off a piece of

soggy cookie with his spoon, tastes it thoughtfully, and pronounces it delicious.

Uncle Wink starts playing the People Game. Of course, I'm the only one who recognizes it.

"I was reading the obituaries just now," he says, "and I was saddened to see an old acquaintance of mine has recently passed on to her reward."

Nobody pays too much attention, but at least we are listening. Especially me. I'm waiting for the punch line.

"Yep. Old Nellie Anderson. She grew up on a farm down in the valley and happened to be the only one present when this duck hatched out of its egg. That darned duck thought Nellie was her mother, and it followed her around for the rest of its life."

"That must have been just duckie," Jamie says as Grandma Noddy passes around the A&W.

There's a slight lull in the conversation until Jamie pipes up again. "Oh, I remember what I wanted to tell you, Mom. You'll never guess who I saw in the library at school last week."

"I give up. Who?" Mom asks, dropping another cookie in her milk.

"Ramona Shumway!"

"Who's she?" I ask.

Mom laughs. "Oh, I remember her, Jamie. The dead bee!"

"Yeah. But you should see her now. She's cut her hair, but she's just as gorgeous as ever. I didn't even know she was going to Cal."

"When Jamie was in the second grade," Mom starts explaining, but Jamie corrects her.

"First grade, Mom," he says. "By the second grade I would have known better."

"Well then, when Jamie was in the first grade, he had such a cute crush on little Ramona Shumway. She lived down the street." Mom looks around the table. "She used to live in the old O'Brien place. Anyway, Jamie wanted to give her some sort of present, and at that time he was fascinated by insects of all kinds."

"A token of my love, actually," Jamie breaks in. "Not just a present. I was trying to tell her I loved her," he says sheepishly, bowing his head in mock embarrassment.

"So he asked me how to spell Ramona," Mom goes on, "and then he painstakingly printed it on an envelope . . ."

"And I put this dead bee inside," Jamie continues, "and left it in her mailbox. She was watching me from her window."

Emery looks over at me and smiles.

Now Mom starts up again. "That afternoon, who's at our door but Ramona's father with little Ramona in tow, eyes all red and teary." Mom laughs. "Jamie had such a time explaining how he thought a dead bee was the ultimate sacrifice at the altar of love."

Uncle Wink laughs, too. "That's beautiful. Reminds me of this guy I used to know in high school named Bryon Foote. He lived in his parents' garage."

Emery begins to stare at Uncle Wink. He doesn't take his eyes off him for a long time.

"Bryon Foote was being chased by a bee once, and he got so excited he climbed on a ladder that was leaning against his garage and jumped off the roof and broke" — he pauses for effect and looks around the table, prompting us with a motion of his hand — "and broke — come on . . ."

"His foot!" we all chorus.

"Nope. Sorry, folks." Wink shakes his head. "Bryon Foote jumped off the garage and broke his hand. Good try, though."

"Good thing his name wasn't Bryon Hand," Jamie says. "He might have broken his tailbone."

We all smile.

"Good thing his name wasn't Bryon Tailbone," Emery says, to my surprise. We all look at him.

"Well, just imagine," he explains with a shrug, "having a name like Bryon Tailbone."

Everyone laughs, but I don't think it's that funny.

Pretty soon I go off to the bathroom and, afterward, passing by Muncie's door, I hear some stirring around in there. I knock and call out to him. "Grandfather? Are you okay?"

There's a response, so I go in. He's sitting on the side of the bed, struggling with his brown sweater. He's got it twisted around, with his arm tangled up in there somehow.

"Oh, here," I say, "let me help."

Helping him, I suddenly think of when Naomi was a two-year-old and how I used to help her with her sweater. Only then it was cute and funny to see her so hopelessly tangled up. Now, Muncie purses his lips, and are his eyes just naturally more watery these days?

We get him straightened around and I help him with his slip-ons and we go slowly through the hall, arm in arm, back to the dining room.

Uncle Wink and my father are sitting next to one another, and I can't help but see how alike their expressions are as they watch us enter the room. Uncle Wink jumps up and gets another chair, and my dad takes Muncie's arm and helps him to his seat. Watching them all, I think about something my grandfather said to me on our way home from that trip to Lake Tahoe so long ago. I remember I had asked him what thoughts had crossed his mind when he had first laid eyes on Winky and Blinky, his little twin baby sons. Was he surprised? Was he pleased? What did he think? Before he answered me, Muncie glanced over at my grandmother Boyd, who was dozing by the window, her head bouncing gently with the movement of the car. Then, imitating her, he waved his arm in the air and whispered to me, "Well, I looked at those two precious babies lying there in their cribs, and I thought, 'Ehh, just arms, and heads.' "

Muncie seems so alone now, sitting next to me at the dining room table. People are talking all around him, but he's staring blankly into space, lost in his own world. I rack my brain, trying to think of something I can say to him. Finally, in desperation, I simply ask, "Well, Grandfather, how was your nap?"

A little bit of the old sparkle shines in his eyes. He

lowers his head and looks at my grandmother Boyd under his bushy gray eyebrows. "Ehh," he says, feebly raising his hand, "just snores and . . . and . . ."

He suddenly looks so distressed and helpless I want to put my arms around him and rock him like a baby.

"And dreams?" I ask quietly. "Just snores and dreams?"

"Yes, yes," he says slowly, almost to himself. "Just snores and dreams, doors and seams . . ." His head nods and I laugh gently, thinking he has made a joke, a play on words. But then I look at his face, his puzzled eyes, and I realize he doesn't even know what he said.

Grandma Noddy pours him half a glass of milk and we finish our dessert. Pretty soon Emery looks at his watch and says he'd better be going. But first he picks up his empty root beer can and looks right at Uncle Wink. "Do you happen to know what they're getting for scrap aluminum these days?"

What a question. I wonder why Emery wants to know that and why he'd ask Wink.

Wink shakes his head. "No, son, I really don't know."

Then Emery starts quoting aluminum prices to Wink — how much it is a ton and what that comes to per can. I can't figure out what's going on.

But Wink listens politely and says, "Hmm. Really? That much, huh?"

"Yup," Emery says, adding significantly, "a friend of mine told me all about it."

Wink looks up, a wee bit more interested now. "A friend of yours?" he asks slowly.

"Yeah. A friend of mine." Emery pauses. "I've known him for quite a long time, actually. He's a one-legged dwarf with a glass eye who plays the sweet potato and lives in a grocery basket."

Wink nearly falls off his chair, and I can't help but look at Emery and smile.

Later that afternoon, Jamie invites Naomi and me to ride to Pasadena while he drives Grandmother Boyd back home, and we both accept. Naomi wants to run home and get our skateboards, since the cement paths in Grandmother's garden are a skateboarder's dream, but it has started to rain.

We pile into the car, me up in front with Jamie, while Naomi and Grandmother Boyd are in the back. Right away my grandmother starts listing the chores she has planned for Jamie. "The batteries in my smoke alarms need changing, and if you could carry some boxes up to the attic for me, and I'm going to need more wood in the wood box . . ."

Naomi is playing around in the back seat, bouncing up and down. "Naomi!" Jamie scolds. "Please sit back and fasten your seat belt."

"Oh, fooey!" she says, frowning at him. "*Okay*." She sits back in her seat with a flounce and starts talking to Grandmother Boyd. I think they're taking about Isadora Duncan, because I hear something about "strangled with her own scarf." Grandmother Boyd used to tell me all about old Isadora, too. She was a famous dancer of the twenties, and Grandmother Boyd met her once. Jamie looks over at me for a second and winks. I guess she used to tell Jamie about her, too.

"Say, Robin," Jamie says now. "You know, I really liked that little guy you brought over this afternoon."

"Emery?"

"You should have heard him while you were gone somewhere. I guess it was when you were helping Muncie."

"Oh yeah? What did I miss?"

Jamie glances in the rearview mirror, checking to see what's happening in the back seat. Naomi and Grandmother Boyd are still chattering a mile a minute.

"Well," Jamie says softly, pointing to the back seat with his thumb, "a certain person made some derogatory comment about welfare — it seems her hairdresser told her another one of those how-come-*they*-drive-Cadillacs-and-eat-steak-every-night-while-we-have-to-work stories — and your friend Emery stood right up to her."

"Oh, God."

"No," Jamie says, almost in a whisper, "it was okay. He was very classy about it. He just interrupted quietly and said maybe he should tell her that he and his mother were welfare recipients and have been for many years."

I sigh, "Oh, jeez."

Jamie laughs softly. "Sure got her attention. I've wanted to argue about that with her for years, but never could work up the nerve. And now this kid comes along and states his case very nicely. Emery told her, in a matter-of-fact way, that his father is dead and his mother is disabled, and although he has had a morning newspaper route and other part-time jobs since he was eleven years old, he can't even begin to support them both on what little he makes."

"Wow."

"I think a certain person might even have learned something, because she did have the grace to say that she didn't mean to imply that they were *all* cheats and bums. But anyway, I wanted to tell you I like the way Emery handled it. Oh, and he also added that he hoped he would be able to repay society someday. I think that's how he put it, 'repay society.' At any rate, the guy's got guts."

I sigh. "He's five feet tall, his mother's a Jehovah's Witness, and now you tell me they're on welfare. God, what a winner."

Jamie gives me an impatient glance. "What do you mean? None of that is his fault. I'm surprised at you. And disappointed, too."

I smile at him weakly, and we ride the rest of the way in silence.

9

It is late morning, three days after Christmas. I have raised only one window shade and I am sitting alone in the darkened front room. Naomi is out somewhere and so is Jamie. Mom is at work, of course, and my dad is heaven knows where.

The house is very quiet. The newspaper is still on the kitchen table, hardly messed up at all. I think about going to get it and maybe reading the comics and Ann Landers, but so far I haven't made a move. I also think about washing my face and brushing my teeth and maybe making some toast, but I just can't seem to get moving. I've been sitting here thinking about a lot of things — April and Bill, the kids at school, and Jennifer and the SRs.

Senior Rally (SR for short) is a bunch of senior girls — actually, they limit it to seven — who are nominated and voted on for membership by the graduating SRs. Jennifer's older sister was one of the founding members. It's not an official school club, of course, but it's the dream of every junior girl to one day be in Senior Rally. Well, I guess I shouldn't say every junior girl. Some kids, the really hopelessly out ones, never seem to care about stuff like that. It might seem like an odd thing to say, but in a way I think I almost envy them. It must be nice and relaxing, not having to worry about being in all the time. The thing is, once you're in, there's nothing worse than being out. Mr. Bussone is definitely against SR. He says it's undemocratic. The kids think that's a funny thing for a dictator to say.

Jennifer's more worried than anyone about making SR next year because of her older sister, and she feels that there's a lot of family pressure. You know, your sister was popular, what's wrong with you? That sort of pressure. Anyway, she's even talked to some reigning SRs about what she can do to improve her chances. I was with her when she was talking to Marla Peters about it. Marla is the chief SR this year. Marla just laughed and tossed her white hair back and said to "think of something spectacular."

One thing the SRs do before they graduate is try to spend a night on top of the Phys Ed Building at school. It's supposed to be a really big deal, but usually the security patrol spots them up there before morning, and they all jump down and scatter and finally end up over at somebody's house. Then they call some of the guys and party until morning. I've never told my parents about that. I don't think they would appreciate it much. At least my mother wouldn't. My father would probably think it was okay until my mother frowned at him and shook her head disapprovingly, and he'd look concerned and say maybe it wasn't such a good idea after all. So I just haven't mentioned it. It'll make it a lot easier in case I decide to join if they don't know about it. That'll be one less lie I'll have to tell. Last year at this time I just *knew* I wanted to be an SR, but now, since I'm feeling so mixed up about everything, I just don't know what I want. I know what I *don't* want, though. I don't want the whole school pointing at me and saying, "There's Robin. She used to be in, but now she's out."

Ever since Marla told Jennifer about doing "something spectacular," Jennifer's been thinking up all sorts of weird schemes, besides asking me for ideas every two minutes, since all of hers have been so off the wall they'd either be impossible to pull off or they'd get us all arrested.

Something attracts my attention out the front window and I glance up to see what it is. It's Bill's brother's pink Pinto.

Bill is alone. He shuts off the motor and just sits there in the car. He must be coming to pick up that bird. And if Jennifer was telling the truth in that note, he may be about to ask me to her party. I suddenly realize that the party is tomorrow.

I quickly wipe my eyes with my fingers, gently removing those sandy little grains of sleep from the corners, and watch Bill from behind the curtain. In a minute he gets out of the car and starts up the front walk. He looks great, as usual. He's wearing faded jeans and a nice dark blue shirt. I wait for him to ring the bell before I go to the door.

"Hi, Bill," I say. "Come in."

"How come it's so dark in here?"

"Oh, I don't know. I guess I just haven't raised all the shades yet. No one's home." I go over and start pulling up the other shades.

"Where are they all?"

"Oh, scattered around."

It's funny, but when Bill's alone, not around the other kids, it's as though he's a different person. Being with the other kids seems to soup him up and make him hyper, turn him into something he isn't. I like him better when he's alone, but I don't know which one is the real Bill.

"I came to get that bird," he says somewhat apologetically.

"Oh, yeah," I answer. "I think it's in Naomi's room. I'll get it."

When I return with the bird, Bill is sitting on the couch with one long leg crossed over, his left foot lying across his right knee. I've never been able to figure out why I so love watching him sit like that.

"I remember the first time I was ever in this room," he says, looking around.

"Oh, really?"

"It was your twelfth birthday party. Remember? Even our old swimming coach was here. What the heck was his name?"

"You mean Ozzie?" I wonder how he could ever forget Ozzie.

"We all went and played miniature golf," Bill says, smiling. "You beat me by five strokes. I've never forgotten that. Then we all came back here afterward. Your father was giving rides."

"Yeah," I say. "I remember that. Gee, everyone was here. Jennifer, Lynnie, David Watson — " I stop short and bite the tip of my tongue. Funny, cute David Watson has been buried for almost six months now at Mount Vernon Cemetery, right down the hill from Tracy Boyd.

Bill turns and looks out the window. I'm still holding the little birdcage, and while Bill's looking out the window, I set it down on the floor at the side of the couch.

"I'm sorry, Bill," I say quietly. "His name just slipped out."

Bill wipes his eyes quickly and says bitterly, "I ran into his mother in the drugstore the other day. She just ignored me. Totally ignored me. You know, that woman still thinks it was my fault."

I just swallow and say nothing.

"I'm sick and tired of defending myself about that. I didn't force him to drink that night. And I wasn't driving, for God's sake. *He* was driving. Everyone conveniently forgets that. Hell, I was lucky I didn't get killed myself." Bill's voice drops. "And I miss him more than anybody," he whispers. "He was *my* friend. Everybody forgets that, too."

I still don't answer. Part of me wants to ask "Well, how come you didn't quit drinking?" But another part of me feels so sorry for him I almost start crying. I murmur an excuse and go into the bathroom and rinse my face and have a drink of water.

When I come out, Bill is still sitting there with his head buried in his hands. I think he might be crying, but I'm not sure. I go over and kneel on the floor at his feet. I reach up and touch his bowed head. "Bill," I whisper, "don't. Please don't. Come on. Please."

Bill stands up slowly and pulls me up beside him. He hasn't been crying. "Robin," he says, rubbing my chin with his thumb, "Jennifer's throwing a party tomorrow night and she thinks — I mean, she's throwing a party and I want you to come with me. How about it?"

I am expecting it, but his timing has caught me by surprise. "I, I don't know," I stammer. "What about April? I thought you and April . . ."

"Let me worry about April," he answers, annoyed. "I'm asking you."

Suddenly the whole scene reappears before me: the same old kids, the laughs, the noise, the music, the crazy jokes. But mostly the friends, being surrounded by friends, and knowing you belong. And then the ride home, Bill's arms, the darkness, being wanted. Gee, Jennifer probably *would* have invited me fourth, just as she said. And I know Lynnie would, and maybe even Michelle. In a crowd as large as mine, there's no disgrace in being fourth.

Bill tightens his arms around me. "Please?"

"Listen, Bill," I say quietly, wanting to get one thing straight between us. "There's something we've already been over a million times. I mean, I'm not going to . . ."

He saves me the embarrassment of getting specific. "For Chrissake, Robin," he whispers, interrupting me and giving my chin a little squeeze. "I'm only asking you to come with me to a party, you know. I'm not asking you to jump into the sack, for God's sake." He says it like it's a big joke. He *is* awfully cute about it.

"Oh, gee. I don't know."

"Please, Robin?" He's stroking my arm. Then he raises his right hand, as if taking an oath. "I promise you I'll behave. Heck, I'm behaving now, aren't I?"

Queen of Hearts, I'm thinking. Just like Lark Greenwillow in Wink's novel. The dream of every high school girl.

"Well," I say. "Maybe . . ."

He takes that to mean yes. "Great! I'll be here around seven-thirty. We'll have a great time. We really will."

After Bill leaves, I go to the kitchen and hunt for something to eat. I remember the banana nut bread in the freezer, so I unwrap it. There are four slices and I drop one in the toaster. When it pops up, I butter it nicely, take a bite, and break a filling in my tooth on a piece of walnut shell.

I feel around in my mouth with my tongue and decide I'd better call Dr. Landis, our dentist. His nurse says he can see me tomorrow at ten in the morning. Just as I hang up the phone it rings, making me jump. It's Emery Day.

"How about a movie this afternoon?" he asks. His voice over the phone is pleasant, deep and clear.

"Oh," I say, hesitating, contemplating an otherwise boring afternoon at home. "Uh, what's playing?"

He tells me about a movie at the Guild, which is a little movie theater not far from here that specializes in foreign films and re-releases. The movie is called A *Little Romance*. I've never seen it.

"Well, okay," I say, winding the cord around my hand and deciding not to tell him I just broke my tooth on his mother's banana bread.

He comes over a little while later, and once again I hop up on the crossbar of his bike. I wonder what the kids would say if they saw me there, riding to the movies with Emery Day.

At the movie, we sit down low and comfortable in our seats, each of us self-contained; not even our elbows touch. The movie is about Young Love and takes place in Europe. The ending is in Venice. It's the first time I have ever seen that city in a motion picture and I am fascinated by its incredible beauty. The movie tells the story of two teenagers (the boy is very short) as they struggle to get to Venice so they might kiss under the Bridge of Sighs at sunset, an action that they believe will seal their love forever.

Emery and I ride back to my house without saying a word. My hair is blowing in the wind and sometimes it touches Emery's face.

I invite him in for a Coke and he accepts. He sits down

at the kitchen table and watches me as I go to the refrigerator.

"I don't like to discuss movies right after I see them," Emery says. "I think it spoils them."

I'm pouring his Coke into a glass when he says that, and I stop pouring and just look at him in amazement. The foam in the glass settles down around the ice, all the little bubbles furiously bursting away.

"That's what I think, too," I say. "That's *exactly* what I think."

I bring the Cokes to the table and sit down across from him. "It's funny it was set in Venice, though, because that's where my grandma's book takes place, at least the ending."

He asks what the book is about, so I tell him a little bit about the plot, and he laughs and says it sounds like a best seller to him.

He takes a swallow of Coke, and I notice that his acne is not really as bad as I thought it was. I count two or three pretty large ones, and around his chin is pretty bad, but I decide it's mostly because he probably shaved that morning. I remember that Jamie always used to complain that shaving wreaked havoc with his zits.

"I was just thinking," Emery says now. "Isn't life strange? Isn't it strange how little things can happen and sometimes change the whole course of your life. And I mean just *little* things."

"I don't know exactly how you mean," I say. "What little things?"

"Well, like a little piece of dust, for instance. If it

weren't for a little piece of dust blowing in my eye on Christmas Day, I wouldn't be sitting here right now. That's a good example of what I mean." He smiles. I notice his smile is as straight as an arrow.

"But you said, 'Change the course of your whole life,' " I point out. "Could it really do that?"

"You never know," he says quietly.

"But then, was it really by chance?" I ask, wondering why I'm enjoying this conversation so much. "I mean, if you knew everything about that piece of dust — you know, how much it weighed, the wind currents that picked it up, where it came from and all that — well, maybe then you'd see that it *had* to be where it was and that it was no accident at all."

The doorbell rings. "I'll get it," Naomi hollers from another part of the house. A few seconds pass. "Robin!" Naomi yells. "It's for you! It's Bill!"

I look up and see Bill standing tall in the doorway, a bronzed god among mere mortals.

"Hi, Robin. It's me again." He notices Emery. "Hey, Day! What the hell are you doing here?" His voice is friendly and warm.

"How you doin', Conyers," Emery says, more like a statement than a question.

"How're you guys doing this year?" Bill asks. I have no idea what he's talking about.

Emery answers, something about some of the guys on the team doing better than they expected.

"What *team*?"

Bill looks at me. "The wrestling team, of course," he says. "Don't you know Day here could take on his weight in barracuda?"

Emery just laughs at that.

Bill has me by the arm now and is sort of pulling me out of the kitchen, at the same time waving at Emery, motioning for him to stay put. "Gotta have a word with Robin, pal. See you around."

Now we're in the front room. "I forgot the goddamn bird."

"Oh, yeah," I say. "It's right here." I pick up the birdcage and hand it to him.

He surprises me with a swift kiss. "Thanks, babe," he says. "Oh, and listen, I was just talking to Jennifer, and she says you're supposed to wear some kind of T-shirt or other."

Just talking to Jennifer? I wonder, but I say, "Yeah. A dirty T-shirt. I already know all about that."

I start to open the front door for him, and there's Wink parking his car behind the Pinto. Wink comes bounding up the steps, and he and Bill exchange a few words. Then Wink goes inside and Bill says, "So I'll see you tomorrow night," and jumps off the low porch, holding the birdcage high in the air. Then he turns and says, as an afterthought, "And listen, take it easy on Day, huh?" He laughs and waves good-bye.

Emery is in the front room when I go back in, and he and Uncle Wink have just shaken hands. It gives me a funny feeling to see them do that, almost as though I'm grown up now, and my friends are no longer just kids.

After they drop hands, Wink gives Emery a good-natured punch on the arm and says, "So how's the price of aluminum today?"

Emery laughs and says, "Well, I guess I'll take off."

"Hey, don't let me chase you away," Wink remarks, flopping into a chair and motioning for Emery to sit down.

Emery looks at me and shrugs, and we both sit down on the couch. Then Wink leans forward and says, "Robin, how'd you like to fly over to New Mexico with me?"

"New Mexico? When?"

Emery looks amazed, but I'm not too surprised. Wink is always flying off somewhere.

"Tomorrow sometime, if the weather holds out."

"Oh, darn. I can't tomorrow. I just promised to go to a party tomorrow night."

Emery looks down at his shoes and brushes the side of his face with his fingers.

"Oh, well, Saturday, then," Wink says. "When do you go back to school? Tuesday?"

"Ugh. Yes."

"We can spend Saturday night in Phoenix and then fly on to New Mexico on Sunday. We should be back by Monday night. I thought Jamie might like to come, too." Wink looks around. "Where is he, anyway? Is he home?"

"No," I say. "He's still out someplace. But what about

Naomi?" I ask, and then I smile. Whenever one of us says, "What about Naomi?" we always think of *The Electric Company* and smile.

"She's not interested," Wink replies. "I've already talked to her about it. I called this afternoon. You weren't home. Anyway, Muffy or somebody is planning a sleepover. They've been planning it since Thanksgiving and Naomi doesn't want to miss it."

"What about Mom?" I ask. "Did she say it's okay?"

"Now, Robin, you know I always clear these things with your mother first."

"Yeah," I admit, "I guess so. But how come New Mexico? What's happening there?"

Wink moistens his lips. "It's for the *Images* book." He looks at Emery. "I've been working on a book of photographs," he explains. "Been at it for quite a while now."

"It's called *From Screen Doors to Wine-Stained Rugs: Present-Day Images of Jesus*," I say.

Emery's eyes widen. "Come again?" he says. But he's got a big smile on his face.

Wink laughs. "It's a slightly unusual title, I'll admit. And if this New Mexico mission pans out, it's going to get even better." He takes his notebook out of his shirt pocket. "You see, uh, there's a little town in southern New Mexico" — he's flipping the pages of his notebook — "ah, here it is. Lake Arthur, population about a hundred. Well, there's a *tortilla* there — a woman fried this tortilla, and when she was done, *voilà!* — an image of Jesus."

"The Jesus Tortilla," Emery says. "I've read about it."

"You're a well-read kid," Wink remarks, a little wind taken out of his sails.

"Not really. It was just in some column or other. Bob Greene, I think it was."

"Well, that's the one," Wink says. "And if it all works out, I'll change the title of my book. How does this grab you? *From Screen Doors to Tortillas . . .*"

"That's even better," I say, and Emery nods in agreement.

"How many photos do you have now?" Emery asks. "For the book, I mean."

"Over two dozen, I guess. But remember, I've been working on this for years. After the screen door, there was the garage door in Santa Fe Springs, the tree in West Virginia, the bathroom floor up in Canada, the wine-stained rug in Dallas — "

"How do you find out about them?" Emery breaks in.

"Oh, on the wire services, usually. And people know I'm interested now, so sometimes I'll get tips from friends around the country."

"That's really amazing," Emery says. "If I hear of any, I'll be sure to let you know." Emery suddenly begins to stare at the drapes. "Wait a minute!" he says slowly. "Look at those drapes over there. Doesn't that — look there, by the tassel — that's his nose, see, and his beard . . ."

"Oh, cut it out, Emery," I say with a laugh.

The conversation sort of slows down, and Emery starts moving his feet around and looking fidgety.

"You're getting ready to leave," I say.

"How'd you know?"

"Well, look at you. Your feet are pointing toward the door. I read an article once that said people do all this body language before they leave. They point their feet toward the door."

He stands up. "Do they stand up, too?"

"That's right."

He starts walking toward the door. "Do they start walking toward the door?"

I stand up, too, and smile. "Thanks for the movie," I say.

"What do you mean? You paid your own way."

That was true. I wouldn't let him pay my way. "Well, thanks for the ride, then."

"Sure. And thanks for the Coke."

Wink's watching us and smiling.

We're at the door now, and I open it as he turns to tell Wink good-bye. "Good luck with the tortilla," he says.

We go out on the porch, but he doesn't leave. He just stands there and looks at me. It's really strange, because I just look right back at him for the longest time. Straight across, right into his eyes, those dark blue eyes with the angry red rims.

"Don't have too much fun at the party tomorrow night," he says, and I think his eyes are going to bore a hole right through me. When he finally turns to leave, I discover I'm covered with a thin layer of perspiration that makes me shiver in the chill of the late afternoon.

10

    I catch the bus at nine-thirty for my ten o'clock appointment at the dentist. I sit in the back of the bus behind two well-dressed middle-aged women and listen to their conversation.

"You mean the lightning struck their *bed?*"

"That's right! Luckily, they weren't in the cabin at the time. They had left a few minutes before the storm broke to hike over to the settlement for a newspaper."

"My gosh. And when they returned their cabin was on fire!"

"The mattress was on fire and smoking to beat the band. But it was funny, too, because Phil and I went running over there, and by that time they were carrying the mattress outside, but they were all wet from the rain, you know, and the feather pillows that were on the bed were ripped open by the fire and feathers were flying all around the room and sticking on them, and by gosh they looked like a couple of chickens."

People all around me are smiling at the story, and I can't get the image of those people — all wet and covered with feathers — out of my mind.

When I get home from the dentist, Jamie asks me if I feel like going to the store with him and picking up some supplies for our trip. Wink has asked him not to forget his Twinkies. Wink can't fly without his Twinkies.

So we go to the store and get some soft drinks and a big bag of ice and Wink's Twinkies. We also buy some Fig Newtons and some apples and bananas.

Once we're back home, I go to my room and start packing my little overnight case. I know I'll get home late from Jennifer's party tonight, and Wink wants to leave early in the morning.

I finally get around to dumping out the bag of books from the Goodwill. There's an old psychology text that looks interesting. Next semester I plan to drop that drama class and take some psychology. I just start looking through the book when the phone rings.

"It's for you, Robin," Jamie calls. "It's Jennifer, I think."

Jennifer wants to know if I'm coming to her party and is overjoyed when I tell her yes. I think she's probably having some kind of feud with April. In fact, I know she is. I think she's using me in some mysterious way to get back at April or something. So far I haven't figured out if Bill realizes there's something funny going on. But the way he smiled at me and told me to take it easy on Day makes me believe he's not all that crazy about me as Jennifer seems to think. All this intrigue is really starting to give me a pain.

"Do you have a T-shirt to wear?" she asks now.

"Not exactly," I say.

"Well, you'd better get one, Robin. I don't want this to end up like that hat party I gave and hardly anyone wore a hat."

"Okay."

She lowers her voice. "I got my stupid parents to agree to bug out."

"Pardon me?" I heard her okay. I just want to see if she'll repeat it.

"I said, Robin, that my mother and father won't be here."

"Oh. That's what I thought you said." Then I add, "Everyone's going to diz out, you know." That's the new slang at our school for getting drunk.

"You think so?" she asks, and then she laughs.

"I've got to go," I lie. "I'm flying somewhere with my uncle tomorrow, so I've got to finish packing."

"Okay. See you later then." She doesn't even ask where I'm going.

After I hang up the phone, I finish throwing stuff in my overnight bag and then I go next door to see Muncie and my grandma. They're sitting in the kitchen having a late lunch.

Grandma Noddy asks me if I'm hungry and I say no, and she says sit down and visit with them, anyway.

She looks pretty haggard. I notice her blouse has some catsup stains on the sleeve, and her hair is flying all over instead of being in its usual neat bun at the back of her head.

"Is everything okay?" I ask softly.

She makes a hopeless gesture and shakes her head. I notice the lines in her face have deepened and her eyes look hollow and bloodshot.

Muncie hardly notices me. All his attention seems to be focused on his silverware. He's turning his fork around and around as if he's never seen it before. Finally Grandma Noddy has to place it properly between his fingers. "This way, Muncie," she says cheerfully. "You remember how to hold your fork."

They're having some potato salad, and he drops most of it on the tablecloth and on his lap. At one point Grandma Noddy tries to help him again, but he angrily slaps her hand away. Finally he scrapes his chair back and lifts himself from the table. He murmurs something like, "Ah, the hell with it," and shuffles off toward his bedroom.

Grandma Noddy absent-mindedly picks up the bits of food around his plate and puts them in her palm. "Oh, Robin," she says, "I just don't know what I'm going to do. He seems to be getting worse so fast." She shakes her head slowly and her eyes well up with tears. "I just never imagined it would end this way."

When I go into the kitchen to put some dishes in the sink, I again notice the calendar hanging on the wall, with the circle around the sixth of January. Now, as each day passes, another number is crossed out with a huge black X.

Well, I don't have a dirty T-shirt. I know Jamie doesn't have one either, but I decide to ask him, anyway. I think what I really want is to talk to him about things.

"Hey, Jamie," I call out, "ever been to a dirty T-shirt party?"

He's in his room, fooling around with his records. His door is open and I can see them all spread out on his bed. Jamie likes classical music, especially baroque. His favorite coffee cup is still the one I gave him a long time ago which has a picture of Bach's face on it and reads, BACH'S MUG.

Now he comes to the doorway of his room and leans up against the doorframe. "What's a dirty T-shirt party?"

"What do you think? Everyone wears a dirty T-shirt."

He shrugs and turns around and goes back into his room. I follow him in. "Jennifer told me she found a really obscene one someplace." I pause. "I can't *wait* to see it," I say with enthusiasm to test his reaction.

I have to laugh at his expression. He looks at me as if he hasn't heard me right.

"Robin," he says finally, "that doesn't sound like you. That's awful."

"Oh no it isn't," I answer lightly.

He goes back to his records, picking one up and examining it for scratches. "What grade are you in, anyway?"

"You know I'll be a senior next year."

He doesn't say anything for a minute. Apparently, he can't find one of his records or something. Finally he snaps his fingers and stoops over and pulls a cardboard box out from under his bed. "Ah," he says under his breath, "here it is." Then he looks up at me. "Can't you find a little higher class bunch to run around with?"

I laugh hollowly, then I get defensive. "They're the most popular kids at school."

" 'Popular?' " he mocks. "Come off it, Robin."

"Well, they are."

He stops what he's doing and looks at me closely. "Is Emery going to be at your dirty T-shirt party?"

"Are you kidding?"

He sighs and goes back to his sorting. "Jesus. Am I glad I'm out of high school."

I just stand around, waiting to see if he's going to say anything else. When he doesn't, I start to leave. "So anyway, do you have a dirty T-shirt or not?" I ask.

He quickly strides over to his closet and opens the door. There's a pile of dirty clothes in the corner. He ruffles through them and picks up a white undershirt with his thumb and index finger and tosses it over to me. "Here, catch!"

I just throw it back at him and laugh, but he's given me an idea.

Bill is late. It's after eight by the time he drives up. I just call out, "So long. I'm going now," and slam the door behind me.

I wonder what Bill will think of my shirt. It's just an old yellow T-shirt I found in my closet, but I messed it all up. I put some chocolate syrup on my hands and then made a couple of handprints on the front, and I spilled a little coffee around and sprinkled some soot from the fireplace on the back. By the time I finished, it was definitely a dirty T-shirt.

Bill is a little slow in catching on, though. At first he thinks the handprints should have been more strategically placed, but then he realizes that they are just supposed to add to the general condition of the shirt, not be the whole point of it. Actually, he doesn't think it's very clever.

I look at his T-shirt then. It's just a large hand with the middle finger raised. Actually, I don't think his is very clever, either.

The car windows are rolled up, but still I hear the music before we even get to Jennifer's house, it's so loud. Bill has to park next door because there are three or four cars ahead of us.

"I see Mike finally made it," Bill remarks, and I realize he has already been at Jennifer's tonight and just left to pick me up. Then I suddenly remember that sentence in Jennifer's note — "I don't know why, but lately he's starting to confide in *me*" — and I begin to wonder what's going on.

Bill and I go up to the door, Bill leading the way, and it bursts open before we get to it and out comes Michelle, running and screaming, followed closely by Mike Soto.

He tackles her on the grass and shoves something down the back of her shirt.

"Say you're sorry," he warns loudly. "Say you're sorry and maybe I'll let you up!"

Michelle is screaming and laughing. He finally lets her up and they start pulling on each other, dragging each other back into the house.

Jennifer gives Bill a big hug when we go in and says something in his ear, but it's such a madhouse and the music's so loud, I can't hear a word she says. God, she's acting like she owns him.

April and a couple of the other kids come over to us and April gives me this really funny look and points to my T-shirt. "What's that supposed to be?" she asks.

"A dirty T-shirt, of course," I answer, but I know by the way she asked the question that she already realizes it's a dirty T-shirt.

Now she turns her head to Randi and says. "That's just like you, Robin," in a really denigrating way, and then she and Randi start to laugh and walk away.

Jennifer and Bill are in the kitchen now, fooling around with the drinks. I join them in there. There's lots of Coke, and some beer, of course, but then I notice a punch bowl filled with red punch. That's something new. I haven't seen a punch bowl at a party since our Kool-Aid and sherbet days.

Jennifer hands a bottle to Bill and he checks the label before he empties the whole thing into the punch bowl. As he tosses the empty bottle into the garbage can, I see that it's Smirnoff vodka, the one that leaves you breathless.

Pretty soon Jennifer goes over and shuts off the stereo. Everyone laughs, because with the stereo suddenly quiet, it becomes apparent just how loudly we've all been shouting to each other. Jennifer calls us all to the front room.

"We're going to go get some pizza," she shouts, "and I want everybody to come."

There are some groans and more shouts, and finally Jennifer holds up her hands and screams, "Shut up!"

Everybody laughs again, but then they shut up, more or less. "So let's all meet at Tony's Pizza," she says. "And listen, when we get there, I want us all to stand up against the counter in a *line*, see? That way, everyone there can see our wonderful T-shirts!"

"Come on, let's go!" Mike Soto shouts.

Everybody scrambles outside, and in a minute car doors are banging and we're on our way to Tony's.

Somehow, I don't know how, Jennifer and Bill are in the front seat of the Pinto, and April, Mike Soto and I are in the back, with Mike in the middle.

"Oh, damn!" Jennifer says suddenly. "I forgot my camera. Go back, Bill."

Bill just keeps driving straight ahead. I could have told her that Bill doesn't like to be ordered around like that.

"Bill! Go back, please! I want to take a picture of everybody in their T-shirts! I want to give it to Marla!" she wails.

"No you don't," Bill says. "That's stupid. Anyway,

there won't be enough light." Bill can be very opinionated, also.

"And what about the flash?" Jennifer asks in that high-pitched voice she sometimes uses. I can't stand her when she gets like that.

Bill just keeps driving. He's not going back. Jennifer slumps way down in her seat and calls him a stubborn bastard.

Suddenly it's very quiet and uncomfortable in the car. We ride along for a little while like that, then Jennifer sits up again and turns around and looks right at me. "Have you thought of anything we could do to impress those SRs yet, Robin? You promised me you'd be thinking about it."

"Oh," I start to say, but April interrupts and says sarcastically, "She can't think of anything. She can't even wear the right kind of T-shirt." And then they all laugh, even Bill.

"Why don't you girls kidnap the Buzzard, or something," Mike Soto says. "You could hold him prisoner until he promises to give back Senior Ditch Day and . . ."

I suddenly remember the conversation I overheard in the bus on the way to the dentist.

"Actually, Jennifer," I say, "I do have an idea."

"I'll bet," April remarks dryly. But Bill says, "Shut up, April. What is it, Robin?"

So I tell them my brilliant idea. I remind them how Mr. Bussone cuts across the west lawn every morning from the parking lot, and how the overhang from the

Shop Building is right at the edge of the lawn. "So here's what you do," I say. "You have someone turn on the lawn sprinklers when he's halfway across. By the time he's over to the Shop Building, he's plenty wet, see?"

"Ohh, *Robin*," April mocks, "that's *so* clever."

"I'm not finished," I say evenly.

"She's not finished, April," Jennifer says. "So what then?"

"Well, he's soaking wet," I continue, "and somebody's hiding on the Shop Building overhang with" — I hesitate slightly, for effect — "with a bag full of feathers. You get a feather pillow, you know, and whoosh — you dump the feathers all over him, and since he's wet . . ." I hold my breath, waiting.

"I love it!" Jennifer exclaims as I exhale slowly. "The feathers will stick to him!"

"The Buzzard!" Mike Soto says. "He'll look like a real buzzard!"

I'm surprised Mike's smart enough to make that connection. Even April agrees, reluctantly, that it's got possibilities.

"I could be on the other side of the overhang," Jennifer adds quickly. "I could take his picture right away, while the feathers are still all stuck to him, and give it to Marla . . ."

"Hey, we could even have posters made," Mike says. "Plaster them all over school!"

"But will it really work?" April asks, examining her nails. "Will the feathers really stick to him? Shouldn't we test it out first or something?"

"We won't know unless we try, will we?" Jennifer says, reaching over the seat and patting me on the leg. "Great idea, Robin! I mean, *really*. I really like that idea!"

Suddenly everything is almost the way it used to be. Those creeping outsider feelings I'd been having recently practically vanish and I feel exhilarated, my mouth moist and my voice loud and confident.

A few minutes later we're all lined up at Tony's, and who should walk in the door but Mrs. Sawyer, my old Sunday school teacher. It takes her about two seconds to read the first couple of T-shirts, and she gets so flustered she almost trips over her own feet. Jennifer's doubled up laughing, and Mrs. Sawyer never does make it to the counter. Bill's middle-finger shirt seems to be the one that finally whirls her around and propels her right back out the door.

Bill's at the counter placing the order, and when it's ready he snaps his fingers impatiently over at Jennifer, who says "Oh!" and pulls a couple of bills out of her pocket and hands them to him. Nobody else offers to pay, but, after all, it *is* Jennifer's party. Her parents gave her the money, anyway, since she doesn't have a job or anything. I've met her parents, of course, and they're really weird. Jennifer's pretty much in control over there. For instance, they're not home tonight. Well, I could probably talk my dad into taking off for the evening, but my mother would only look at me and say something like, "Fat chance, kid." I suddenly feel very sorry for Jennifer.

Bill hands a couple of the pizzas over to me —

they're all boxed up, of course — and also gives some to Jennifer, and when we get to his car, old April jumps right into the front seat before I even get to the door. Bill's all hyper, as usual, and doesn't even seem to notice who's sitting next to him. From the way Jennifer's glaring at April, you'd think *she* was Bill's date instead of me, for God's sake. Naturally, I don't make any waves about it, unlike Jennifer, who gives April this really killing look and then disgustedly flops down in the back seat, accidentally dropping one of the pizza boxes on the floor of the car.

"Damn," she says, and I pick it up as I squeeze into the seat beside her.

We don't see Mike anywhere and Bill doesn't even wait for him. He just starts the motor and takes off. I look out the back window and see Mike standing at the curb, shouting and waving his arms, and somebody — I think it's Adam Carlson — makes a U-turn right in all that traffic and goes back after him, tires screeching all around.

"Where's my change?" Jennifer demands. I can tell she's still mad about sitting in the back.

"What do you mean, *change?*" Bill answers. "You owe me five bucks, for God's sake."

"I thought I gave you two twenties."

"Well, how much do you think it was, birdbrain? What's six times seven-fifty?"

"I don't know." Jennifer pauses. "Well, I'll pay you back later," she says. Then she starts being cute and says it again, with little sexy overtones: "I'll pay you back later, Bill baby," something like that, and April turns around and stares at her. Jennifer sticks her tongue out at April, and suddenly they both burst out laughing. It's really strange to see them laughing like that, since they're always competing with each other. I don't know what's going on.

It's almost midnight when the funny stuff starts. I've been mostly pretty bored all evening, except when Muriel Monroe and I were rinsing out some glasses in the kitchen. Even though Muriel's awfully quiet, I've always liked her. She's supposed to have a boyfriend over at Caltech this year, but I've never seen him. While we were in the kitchen, she was telling me about this theory she has that there is only one homemade fruitcake in the world, and people just keep passing it around to each other at Christmastime. She said her mother just got it today from a friend at work, and then she passed it right on to their next-door neighbor. Muriel and I are the only ones who haven't had any of that punch, even though everyone kept asking us to and asking us why we didn't.

I know it's almost midnight, because after I finish drying the last glass I happen to glance at the clock over the stove. It's in the shape of a little kitten and its tail is wagging like a pendulum.

I hadn't spent too much time with Bill the whole evening. We did sit on the floor near each other while we ate our pizza, but then he disappeared for a while, and later I saw him in a little huddle with Mike and April and Jennifer. They were acting very mysterious and stupid, so that's when Muriel and I went to the kitchen and started doing the glasses.

Anyway, Muriel and I finish in the kitchen and wander toward the front room. Some kids have paired off now, and I think some are upstairs, since the stairs aren't carpeted and it's really noisy when people go up and down. It sounds like the whole house is going to fall apart.

Muriel and I are walking through the dining room and I suddenly feel myself being lifted into the air in a mad scramble of hands and elbows. Muriel is bumped so hard her glasses fly off. I hear her shout, "Hey! Quit it!" Then, "Watch out, you're going to *step* on them!"

Somebody sticks an oversize baseball cap on my head and yanks the visor down over my eyes. I can't see how many people are carrying me, but whoever has my leg is practically twisting it off its socket. Everything is happening so fast, and there is so much noise and confusion. I know they're taking me upstairs, and I can hear Jennifer's high-pitched voice calling, "Up here!" And I know now the person who has me by the shoulders is Bill Conyers.

I've stopped struggling now, since it only made them hold me more tightly and I could see I was only hurting myself.

"Don't turn on the hot water," someone says urgently. "You might scald her."

"Just the cold water, Mike!"

And I realize what they're doing. I'm getting showered. I've heard about kids getting showered for years; even

Jamie used to talk about it. But it's supposed to be all in fun. It's supposed to be good-natured and fun. It's not supposed to be like this.

A dozen hands pass me in, and the shower door is closed and held shut and I fumble for the faucets, my breath suddenly taken away by the cold torrents of water. Before I find the knobs, the door opens and I'm yanked out. The kids are laughing and yelling and jumping all around, but since they're so rough with me, I feel as though I'm in the middle of a war.

I don't quite know what's happening, except that they're still holding me, and now I'm dripping wet and shivering. My shoes are full of water and squishing all over the floor.

Suddenly I hear Jennifer scream, "Not in the *house*, you bozos!" and at the same time I'm engulfed by a huge cloud of little white feathers.

Everyone's screaming now — I can hear April's voice: "It works! It works! Look how they stick on her!" — and the kids are running all around and I fall, and I can hardly see because even though I snatch the cap off my head, I'm still surrounded by millions of flying feathers.

Then there's a thunderous roar. They've all run down the stairs and I'm left alone, sprawled out at the top of the stairs, crying and covered with feathers.

I've never felt such humiliation and pain. The kids are all downstairs now, taunting me with bird whistles and calls of "Fly, Robin! Fly!"

I long to take it all good-naturedly. I want to laugh and pretend to fly down the stairs and join them all there in a warm circle of friendship. But it's all wrong. My "friends" have all disappeared. I'm being ridiculed, and I feel alone and betrayed. They didn't like my T-shirt and I wouldn't drink the punch. I've been passing judgment for weeks, and the crowd has turned on me at last.

Suddenly I'm thinking very clearly. I remember the fire escape ladder in Jennifer's room. I stand up and make a dash for her room, slamming and locking the door behind me. I open her window and throw out the rope ladder and I'm outside and on the ground before I know what's happening. I take off down the street and turn in the alley. I know there's a 7-Eleven two blocks away with a pay phone outside by the news racks. I run all the way without stopping. I take some change from my pocket and call Jamie, and he comes right over and drives me home.

11

I've been in Wink's plane I don't know how many times, but I'm still nervous whenever we take off. It's a red and white Cessna 172, a four-passenger job that cruises at about 130 knots.

As usual when Jamie's along, I sit in the back. Jamie puts on the spare headset and listens to the conversation between Wink and the tower.

It's noisy in the plane's cabin, but after a while my ears adjust and I settle back with the ice cooler and snacks, a couple of magazines and *The Scarlet Letter*. Jamie and Wink are talking to each other through their headsets, but I can't hear them. I watch the scene below for a while, the fields and roads and treetops and rivers. I smile to myself as I think what Muncie would say: "Ehh, just sky, and ground."

Pretty soon I close my eyes, and my mind drifts back

to Jennifer's party. I rush through the awful parts and remember what happened when Jamie came to pick me up. He was so great. All he did at the 7-Eleven was jump out of the car and ask me first thing if I was okay.

"Yes," I said, "I'm okay." My throat felt scratchy and sore, and I realized I must have been screaming a lot over there.

"What's that stuff all over you?" He picked a couple of feathers off my T-shirt. "It looks like feathers."

"It is." Most of them had blown off by then, though.

He let that sink in for a second, and I thought he was going to ask some more questions, but he didn't. "Well," he said simply, opening the trunk and pulling out an old blanket. "Here, wrap up in this so the feathers won't fly all over the car."

"All right."

"You're sure you're okay now? Where's Bill?"

"Bill? Oh, he's still there, I guess."

"Listen, Robin, I don't want to butt into your business, but have you ever thought about dropping out of that crowd?" Jamie asked, stealing sideways glances at me. "It just seems to me that some of those kids have changed a lot since the old days at Three Oaks."

"I don't want to talk about it now, okay?"

Jamie shrugged, and that's all we said.

When we got home, I went into the bathroom and stood on the blanket and shed my clothes on it and rolled it all up like a sleeping bag. Then I took a hot shower and went to bed.

I couldn't sleep, though. My heart kept beating about twice as fast as usual, like before my tonsillectomy, when I used to have terrible sore throats and my temperature would go up to 103.

An hour or so after I was in bed, the phone rang. I ran to get it and answered it at the same time my mom picked up the extension in her room.

"Hello, is this Robin?" a girl's voice asked softly.

My mom made some sort of unintelligible reply, and I said slowly and distinctly, "It's okay, Mom. It's for me." and she hung up, banging the receiver on her night table.

"Oh, God, I woke up your mother. Robin, this is Muriel."

"Oh," I said. "Hi."

"I . . . I wanted to call and make sure you got home okay and everything."

"I'm home."

"Well, I was just kind of worrying, since you . . ."

For some unknown reason, I started to cry.

"Robin?"

I couldn't answer. I didn't want her to know I was crying.

"Robin, are you still there?"

"Uh-huh."

"Well, I don't think they really knew what they were doing, you know? They were drinking a lot and just got carried away. After you left, well, some of the kids started saying they thought April and those guys played a dirty trick on you and . . . Robin?"

"Yeah."

"And anyway, I don't think they meant to . . . well, you know. Robin?"

"Huh?"

"Well, okay then. So, I guess that's all. I'll see you at school on Tuesday. The vacation sure went fast, didn't it? Well, it's pretty late. I'd better hang up . . ."

I wanted to thank her for calling, but I couldn't. I just said, "Bye," and we both hung up.

Wink turns to me and tells me he's ready for his root beer and Twinkie, so I fix cold drinks for us and we have a little snack. After that, I read an article in an old magazine Wink has back here. It's about Prince Charles. Someone quoted him as saying that sometimes when he thinks about being the King of England, it blows his mind. He wonders, *How come out of all the people in the world, I have been born the future King of England?* It's a good article. Prince Charles really seems like a nice guy.

Pretty soon we arrive in Phoenix. The weather is perfect, clear and mild with just a slight westwardly breeze. Wink gasses up the plane while Jamie and I go to a phone booth and call a cab.

We go to the little motel Wink always stays at whenever he's in Phoenix. We even get the same room we had the time we went to the Grand Canyon and stopped here on our way over. It's a two-room suite, so I get a room all to myself.

It's early afternoon by now. Wink says he's got a few

errands to do and will be back for us later, then we'll go for an early dinner.

So Jamie and I watch this really stupid movie on TV about some prehistoric monster that takes over the world. His name is Karmack, and he loves to eat metal. Some of those movies are so dumb they're funny, but this one is just dumb.

Wink returns just as Karmack is starting to devour Detroit, and we don't even mind shutting it off.

"I've got a little surprise for you, Robin," Wink says. "Put on your shoes and let's go."

Apparently, Jamie is in on the secret. I hear the two of them talking quietly while I'm in the other room.

"The place we're going to is about two miles from here," Wink says when I'm ready. "So we'll take a cab over, and then we can have dinner and walk back. How does that sound?"

"Fine," Jamie says, and I nod my approval.

Wink picks up the phone to call for the cab.

"So where are we going?" I ask Jamie.

Wink shushes me while he gives the address of the motel to the cab company. Then he hangs up and says, "Well, I was talking to Mrs. Ruggles down in the office, and she was telling me that the old Prescott mansion is on the market again. Her sister works for Higgins's Properties, and they happen to be handling the sale."

"So, what's the Prescott mansion?" I ask.

"You've never heard of it?"

"No. Should I have?"

"My goodness. What do they teach you kids in school

nowadays? Well, I'll tell you about it on the way there. Let's wait for the cab over by the office."

A few minutes later the cab arrives, and Wink runs over and says a few words to the driver while Jamie and I are getting in. The driver just nods his head and Wink goes around and gets in the passenger side.

Then Wink tells me something that practically knocks my socks off. In the year 1866, when she was thirty-four years old, Louisa May Alcott and her father took a trip west on the train, traveling on the brand-new Pullman Sleeping Car.

"As you know," Wink remarks, "the Pullman car was invented in 1859."

"Well, actually, I had forgotten that little piece of trivia." I smile.

"Well," Wink continues, "everyone knows that Louisa's father was a very good friend of Emerson and Thoreau, but he also served in the Union Army with a certain William Prescott, a young reporter from — "

"Wasn't he the founder of the Prescott newspaper chain?" Jamie interrupts, rubbing his upper lip with his fingers.

"That's right. Anyway, the Alcotts, father and daughter, were invited to spend the summer months of 1866 in the Prescott family mansion here in Phoenix while the Prescotts went abroad, and, feeling that his daughter could certainly use a break from the hard routine of New England life . . ."

"Yes, go on. Go on," I say, starting to get a little tingle all over my body. "So did they really come? Were they here in Phoenix?"

"That they were," Wink says. "They came out here late in June, and it's said that Louisa actually began work on *Little Women*, taking notes and so forth. Ah, driver!" he says suddenly. "Just let us off here, please."

The driver touches the top of his cap in a kind of salute and pulls to the curb. Wink pays him and I hear the driver say, "Why thank *you*, sir!"

"My God," I whisper to Jamie as we wait on the sidewalk. "Do you realize what's about to happen? Do you realize I'm about to go into a house that Louisa May Alcott was in! I can't believe it!"

"So what's the big deal?" Jamie asks, yawning. But I know he's just teasing me.

We're standing under a huge elm tree in a quiet, more or less rundown residential neighborhood. The sidewalk is humped and cracked, and there is hardly any traffic. Wink points halfway down the block to a huge brown house with a wide porch and a shady, overgrown yard. "That's the place," he says. A sign posted on the lawn reads: HIGGINS'S PROPERTIES — OPEN HOUSE TODAY, 2 TO 5 P.M.

I'm simply enchanted by the house. The brown shingles seem to sing out "Louisa!" and the lovely front steps have spooned-out indentations where *her feet* have trod.

Wink has gone on ahead, and I see him through the old-fashioned front window, talking earnestly with the real estate woman.

The front door is open and I walk in as if I'm entering a cathedral. A circular staircase seems to dominate the front parlor, and the house smells like something out of another age, romantic and mystical. I can almost feel Jo March in that room.

I'm startled to hear the antique clock on the mantel chime three times, and I'm filled with wonder as I imagine that Louisa herself probably heard that very same sound.

I walk through the charming dining room, with its glassed-in cupboards painted an old-fashioned shade of green, and go into the roomy kitchen. *She might have washed dishes in this very sink.* I look out the small window above a storage area. *She looked out this very window.*

On the way back to the parlor I examine the walls and ceiling. The wallpaper is slightly faded with age, but its former beauty is still visible just below the surface. I reach out and touch it gently with my fingertips and I'm overwhelmed by an indescribable feeling of joy and awe.

"Go upstairs, if you like," the real estate lady suggests. I touch the wooden banister, and something like a burst of electricity surges through my body. I find myself gliding up the stairs as if in a trance. *Louisa May Alcott touched this banister and walked on these stairs.*

It's the most beautiful staircase in all the world, with its graceful curve and landing alcove placed midway between the floors.

I walk into one of the bedrooms and I just *know* it is the one in which she slept. Her aura is unmistakable.

The others are coming up the stairs now. I go out to meet them, but the expression on Wink's face tells me that something is terribly wrong.

"Oh, what's the matter?" I ask, alarmed, thinking that he must be suddenly ill.

He puts his arm around my shoulder. "There's been a mistake, Robin," he says gently. "A terrible mistake. This is *not* the house we were looking for."

"What do you *mean*?"

His voice is soft and understanding. "The Alcott house is several blocks from here. I just saw the Higgins's Properties sign and naturally thought that this was the place. I'm so sorry, dear, but I didn't think to check the house number."

The real estate woman is nodding her head and motioning awkwardly with her arm. Then they go back downstairs, leaving me alone in the bedroom where I had thought for sure Louisa May Alcott had slept.

I'm suddenly overwhelmed by a phenomenon so strange and singular, I know it will live in my memory forever: in the wink of an eye, a beautiful and magical old home becomes an ugly firetrap, badly in need of repair.

I begin to retrace my steps, and I notice how ineptly the staircase landing is placed. The banister wobbles, and the squeaking stairs themselves are uneven and dirty. Reaching the entrance to the dining room, I glance inside and am amazed at how a once "old-fashioned" shade of green paint now borders on the putrid. The wallpaper is dingy and stained, and the whole house smells like mildew.

Wink and Jamie are standing on the porch and I go outside to meet them. I look at the dead rosebushes and tall weeds in the side garden which weren't there a few moments ago, and I notice that the brown siding shingles are really some sort of cheap synthetic. We cross over the spotty lawn and make our way back to the sidewalk.

"Let's go have some dinner," Wink suggests with an understanding smile, "and talk about reality."

"Congratulations," Wink tells me later over our milkshakes and cheeseburgers. "You have now experienced at first hand what I call a PIP. The Proust Incident Phenomenon. I'll explain to you in a minute how it all came about," he adds, "but first, I've got another surprise."

"I think I've had enough surprises for one day, thank you," I say, trying not to sound as disappointed as I'm beginning to feel.

"No." He smiles. "This one you'll like. I've checked the dates for your spring vacation — it comes early this year, at the end of March."

"Yes. Go on."

"And I've also checked with your parents, and the plan is that we're all going to spend four days on the East Coast." He pats my arm reassuringly. "And that's *real* Alcott territory, honey. I've got an okay from my editor to do a special story on her, and you can come along every step of the way. Whatever there is to see, we'll see." He sticks out his hand. "Fair enough?" he asks. "Am I forgiven?"

I shake his hand with my right one and wipe my eyes with my left.

"Now then," Wink says, "about this famous Proust Incident Phenomenon — "

"But wait, Wink," I say. "Hold it. You told me back there that you just had the wrong house, that the real Alcott house was just down the block. Now you say there is none here in Phoenix at all, that you made the whole thing up. I don't understand. Why did you tell me then that you just had the *wrong* house?"

"Ah-ha!" Wink exclaims. "Very simple. If I had told you while you were upstairs in that house that I had simply lied to you, you would have been so incensed, you wouldn't have been able to experience the full PIP effect. As it was, you just thought I had made a mistake, so your unique experience of having an entire house change its personality before your very eyes was not marred or diminished by anger toward me."

I sigh and nod. "Oh, I see. That's very clever, Uncle Wink. You think of everything."

"You're not mad, are you, Robin?" Jamie asks.

"Oh, no. Not if I get to see the real thing in a couple of months. And I must admit, that PIP or whatever you call it, Wink — well, it was quite an experience. It was just like you said — an entire house *did* change right before my eyes."

"I know exactly how you're feeling," Jamie says. "Wink gave me my PIP a couple of years ago." He laughs. "It had something to do with Farrah Fawcett."

"I had the original PIP many years ago," Wink starts to explain. "I was just nineteen, an eager young American seeing Paris for the first time. In those days I was as enamored of Marcel Proust, the famous French novelist, as you presently are of Louisa May Alcott."

He leans back in his chair and wipes his mouth with his napkin. "Actually, you know, I've been wanting to do this for a long time, giving you your own PIP, I mean, but it wasn't until Christmas Eve that the idea of using Louisa May Alcott finally dawned on me. Remember how we were talking about her that night?"

I nod indulgently. "Yep. I remember all right."

Wink smiles at Jamie and continues. "Anyway, as a young man in Paris, I happened to find myself in an old building I thought was once the home of my hero, Marcel. To make a long story short, I toured that building with such a feeling of awe, only to learn later that Marcel Proust had nothing whatever to do with it. I was extremely disappointed at first, as you were, Robin. But later I began to see that I had learned a really invaluable lesson about the true nature of things, about how so much of what we think we see is merely the result of our own longings and desires."

As I am pondering that statement, a young woman — a girl, really — has approached our table. She is wearing a loose-fitting yellow dress belted softly at the waist. She smiles sweetly at Jamie and holds out a flower to him. She is asking him to buy the flower. I think she is a Moonie.

Jamie is embarrassed and shakes his head. A friend walks up now and joins her. "Jesus loves you," her friend intones, holding out a flower of her own and looking right at Wink.

"Thank you," Wink says, but he doesn't take the flower.

"And He died for you."

Wink nods. "I appreciate that. Dying is a terrible thing."

We ignore the girls then, turning away and resuming our conversation, but they don't go away. I begin to feel uncomfortable and Jamie coughs nervously into his hand.

The girls hold out their flowers to Wink again. "No, thank you," he says softly, but the girls persist.

"Yes, indeed," Wink says now, his jaw firmly set. "Dying is a terrible thing. And the really awful thing about it is that it's so permanent."

Wink's eyes start to shine, and Jamie looks at him with a squint, at the same time kicking me gently under the table.

The girls are smiling and nodding their agreement. "Otherwise," Wink continues, "death is not much different from sleep. But that relentless *permanence*, that is what makes the difference."

"And He died for you," the first girl repeats, holding out her palm expectantly.

Uncle Wink suddenly sits bolt upright and raises his hand. "But hold it! Just a gol-derned minute! Jesus didn't *stay* dead, did He now? He died for us, it's true, but then He rose again! He came back to life!"

The girls are looking confused and they take a step backward, but there is no stopping Wink. "So what's the big deal?" he asks, standing up now and feigning indignation. "What *is* the big deal, huh? He didn't stay dead, now, did He? He might just as well have taken a nap, for pity's sake!" He's shaking his fist in the air.

The girls are backing away now, touching each other for support, not knowing what to think of this madman. "But don't forget how he suffered," the older one says, her voice quavering.

"Have you ever been in a cancer ward, my dear?" Wink asks. "Have you ever seen a child afflicted with cystic fibrosis?" But Wink's questions are rhetorical, because the girls are near the door now, and I don't think they hear him.

Wink sits down again, and we all settle back and look at each other.

"Wink," I say finally, "you're really something, you know that? First you come up with something you call a PIP, and then you tell a couple of Moonies that Jesus might just as well have taken a nap."

I smile at Jamie in spite of myself, and Wink grins at us and says, "Come on, you two. We'd better go get some rest. There's a Jesus Tortilla somewhere in New Mexico waiting to be photographed, and our mission is to go out there and find it."

The Jesus Tortilla turns out to be a major disappointment. We finally locate it in a little bungalow in Port Arthur, after renting a car in Carlsbad and poring over the road map. We miss seeing the famous caverns, though, because the long-range weather forecast looks bad, and Wink says we have to get out of there before the storm hits.

"Not on *my* account," I joke. "I don't have to hurry home. I can miss all the school I want."

Wink says that's fine, but he needs a day to pack. He's going to take Muncie and Grandma Noddy to Venice for three days, and they're leaving on Thursday.

About the Tortilla, well, the image of Jesus is about as big as a walnut, and to me it looks more like a spider. But the people there are nice enough and the Tortilla is suitably displayed, enclosed in a glass case and surrounded by plastic flowers. Wink politely asks permission to photograph it, both with his Polaroid and his regular camera, and is answered by polite nods. We don't laugh or act silly. We leave a small donation and beat it out of there quickly.

In the plane on the way home I take out the psychology book from the Goodwill, and I read about peer pressure and social adjustment, which makes me think about the in crowd and all the doubt and confusion I've been having lately about my own friends. The psychology book says that peer pressure is one of the most powerful forces in the life of a teenager. The need to belong, to be like the others, to be accepted by the group — all these things exert such pressure on most young people that their sense of values and their innermost moral convictions often fall by the wayside.

My God, I think, that's exactly what's been happening to me. All of a sudden, there in the cabin of Wink's airplane, I experience another PIP. The kids who have been my friends for years have been tried and found wanting; just because they're in does not mean they're the best.

Pretty soon Wink turns around in his seat and taps me on the shoulder. "Look here," he says, showing me the Polaroids he took of the Jesus Tortilla. "This thing looks better upside down!"

We arrive back home at about three in the afternoon on New Year's Eve. My mom is in a dither because Grandmother Boyd has asked her if she will come over right away and help her get ready for a small party she's giving for some of her bridge club lady friends.

"On New Year's Eve!" Mom exclaims. "Cripes!"

"Can we come along?" Naomi asks. She looks at me eagerly. "We can go skateboarding, Robin. Do you want to?"

That sounds good to me. After being cramped up in the plane for so long, skateboarding sounds like fun. "Sure," I say. "Let's go."

"Well, we're certainly not staying too long, girls," Mom says. "I'll just help her put up the tables and set out the dessert dishes and that's it."

The sun is just beginning to set as we pull in my grandmother's tree-lined drive.

She's in a pretty jolly mood, in contrast to my mom, who tries to hide her irritation, however, and calmly asks how many ladies are expected. I wonder how the pattern started, with Mom always buckling down to Grandmother Boyd and Tracy always rebelling.

Naomi and I head for the back door, and my grand-mother calls out, "Turn on the floodlights out there, Naomi, dear." When Naomi and I are here together, my grandmother always singles out Naomi's name. In this case, Naomi can't even reach the light switch, since it's in a little fuse box high up on the porch wall. I flip it on, and instantly Grandmother's backyard park becomes alive with lights and shadows. I can't help but think how obvious it is that Naomi is my grandmother's favorite. It used to hurt my feelings, but now I've come to understand it: I must remind her of Tracy.

After a few minutes of skateboarding, I try to make the difficult curve by the fish pond and land on my face instead.

Naomi comes right over. "Oh, gee!" she says. "You're bleeding! Your chin is bleeding and your nose is all scratched up."

She helps me up and we go back to the house. Mom and Grandmother Boyd are busy in the kitchen. I brush past them and go right to the bathroom. I quickly splash water on my face and rinse off my hands. "Ouch," I mutter. "That stings." I grab a towel off the rack and press it to my chin.

"Oh, Robin!" my grandmother exclaims, peering in through the bathroom door. "Not the *guest* towel, for land's sake." She opens a drawer in the hallway and passes me a regular towel. "Here now, use this."

Grandmother Boyd returns to the kitchen and says something in a loud voice about the back porch door being left open, something sarcastic about how Robin always leaves the back porch door open, thereby heating up the entire neighborhood.

Naomi is standing next to me, and since she is the one who left the door open, she just looks at me and shrugs helplessly. Then she walks over and closes the back porch door. "I left it open, Grandmother," she says. "Sorry."

"Oh," my grandmother says. "Oh. Well, thank you for closing it, my dear."

Naomi signals to me behind our grandmother's back and then does such a great pantomime of a spoiled child lording it over the unfortunate one that we both come down with the giggles.

12

Tuesday morning, and it's raining. Christmas vacation is over, so it's back to old Southside High for another dose of the happiest days of my life.

I don't know what to expect from my so-called friends. If it weren't for Muriel's phone call that night after Jennifer's party, I probably wouldn't even want to face them at all.

Wouldn't you know, the first person I see is April Maye. Her father has double-parked his white El Dorado and she steps out and slams the door without even saying good-bye to him. I'm crossing the street two feet ahead of her, so I know she sees me. I have a split second in which to decide whether to turn and greet her or just walk on and ignore her, a split second in which to decide whether I'm going to cave in and grovel just to stay in the crowd or say to heck with them all, and be a friendless outcast, an object of curiosity and pity, the girl who no longer belongs.

I quickly turn and look at her. It's still raining, but not hard. April is holding a notebook over her head and looking over her shoulder, checking for cars. Our eyes meet and she smiles. "Hi, Robin," she says, a cat playing with a mouse. "Did you have a nice Christmas?"

Even though I've learned to distrust that smile, her apparent friendliness has disarmed and confused me. Could it be that she's repentant?

"I guess so," I reply. "How about you?"

She starts rattling off all the presents she got as we cross the street and hurry up the steps. I reach the door first, so I swing it open for her. She even says thank you as she walks through, then she holds the door for me. We have entered through the west wing, over by the auditorium. Michelle is standing by the trophy case with Bill Conyers and Mike Soto. It's sort of a gathering place for us. Marla Peters and the other Senior Rally girls hang out around the bench right across the hall from the trophy case. No one but an SR girl would ever dream of sitting on that bench.

In a few minutes Jennifer and Randi show up, then Kathy and some of the other kids.

As usual, April and Jennifer are monopolizing the conversation, trying to outshout each other. The circle of kids has drawn closer, and I find myself struggling for an opening, actually pushing Michelle to one side so I can hear what they're saying. Michelle gives me a really dirty look and pushes me back. "Hey, watch it, Robin!" she says, and elbows me again sharply.

I notice something funny: Jennifer and Bill are holding hands. April notices it, too, and makes some remark about it, and suddenly there's one of those unexplained silences that sometimes happens in crowds.

Bill looks right at April and pulls Jennifer closer to him with a defiant grin. Then Jennifer puts her arms up around his neck and gives him a big kiss. Still looking into his eyes, she says triumphantly, "Congratulate us, April. We're going steady."

The news seems to floor April, but it hardly fazes me. In fact, it really explains a lot of things. And after what they did to me at Jennifer's party, I'm thoroughly shock-proofed as far as treacherous acts are concerned.

Of course, everyone's looking at April now, watching for her reaction. I know April well enough to tell when she's upset. She's upset now, that's for sure. But she's good at hiding it. She's the kind of person who can smile even when everything goes wrong. She's smiling now, looking around the crowd, and her face is only slightly flushed.

Her eyes stop at mine. "Well, what are *you* looking at, Robin? And what happened to you, anyway? Your nose looks disgusting. You been flying around again and land on your face or what?" And she laughs hollowly.

April has managed to squeeze out of a potentially embarrassing position once again, this time by using me as a decoy. The kids are all laughing at me now, not at her.

I'm saved by the bell, however, as the warning buzzer for first period echoes down the hall.

The kids are acting really strange now. Outwardly, they are polite to me — too polite, actually. I catch some behind-the-hand smirks, and during World History April refers to me as a "goody-goody." Lynnie Jeffries wasn't at the party, and so April is telling her about it, saying that most people wore really cute T-shirts, except me. And mine was so stupid it wasn't even funny. "And she wouldn't even drink the punch," she adds.

I usually don't like history that much, but I find today's lesson very enlightening. We're talking about the chapter on prewar Germany and how Hitler used the Jews to galvanize the German people. Having something to hate unified them, gave them a common purpose. I realize that's just how April is using me.

As for Jennifer, she finally has what she was after all along, and that's Bill. She hasn't said two words to me all morning, and that really hurts. I realize now that our friendship has finally run its course. It's funny, but for a while all I can think about is that beaded Indian friendship ring in the miniature cedar chest at home. The only way I keep myself from crying is remembering how the last time I tried to put it on, it wouldn't even fit my little finger.

The rest of the kids continue to ignore me, and by third period, I've definitely decided that I'll walk barefoot through burning coals before I'll sit in the cafeteria with that bunch of jerks.

Lunch period finally arrives, and according to my plan, I don't even go to the cafeteria. First, I go to my locker and stash the books from my morning classes. Then I start walking down the corridor. My stomach is churning so badly I'm not even thinking clearly. Besides, I can no longer hold back the tears.

For no reason at all, I find myself heading toward the girls' gym. I decide I'll go to the little lavatory near Miss Jacobs' office and lock myself in a stall. On the way over there, a couple of people say hi to me, but they are only acquaintances, not friends. You don't ask acquaintances if they will sit and have lunch with you.

I get over to the lavatory and go into a stall and lock the door, intending to pull myself together. What happens is absolutely the reverse: I fall apart.

Pretty soon I hear two girls come in, and I don't know if I know them or not. They are talking about somebody named Shelley. I don't recognize their voices and I don't know anyone named Shelley, so I probably don't know them, either. I just stay put until they leave, and then I blow my nose and flush the toilet and go over and wash my hands. I look at my watch and realize that I have used up only ten minutes of my lunch period. That leaves twenty-five minutes to go. I walk out the side door by the gym and head out toward the tennis courts. The rain has stopped, but the walks and grass are still wet. Then I walk all the way back to my locker and look at my watch again. Three more minutes have passed.

I've never been to the library during lunch hour; I'm

not even sure it's open. I decide to walk over there, the long way, and check it out.

About ten people are there, most of them sitting alone. I don't know any of them. There aren't any empty tables, so I sit across from a girl who's wearing a really ugly brown nubby-knit coat. She's slumped way down in her seat reading a paperback, and I notice that her fingers are full of warts. From time to time she picks at her nose and makes really disgusting snuffing-up sounds.

I go to the nearest shelf and pull out a book and come back to my seat, pretending I've got some very important studying to do. I can't even see the words, though, because my eyes are starting to puddle up again. I cover my face with my hands and order myself not to cry.

What am I doing here? I think desperately. What am I doing here? — a loner, sitting in a library surrounded by misfits. And then — oh my God, it hits me! — I'm turning out to be just like my aunt Tracy, and I can't do a thing about it.

After a time, I sense the warmth of someone standing at my shoulder. As I turn my head, I see the Levi's vest and blue plaid shirt. It's Emery Day. He extends his hand to me, knuckles up and fist clenched. I don't understand what he's trying to do. He looks at me impatiently and says gruffly, "Give me your hand." I still don't understand. So with a quick gesture he lifts my left hand from the table and turns it palm up, at the same time releasing the contents of his own clenched fist. Then he turns and walks away as I look down to see what he's given me. I open my palm to find a handful of red hots, still warm from his touch. I can't begin to explain how it makes me feel.

Apparently no one misses me at lunch, and Jennifer and I avoid each other during Gym. During drama class I catch Muriel staring at me, but when our eyes meet she quickly turns away, as if I'm contagious. At one point I take a little wallet calendar that I got at the dentist's office out of my purse and study it diligently, as if I'm checking for an important date, but what I'm really doing is counting the weeks until the spring break, just like Mr. Wallace.

The three-thirty buzzer finally sounds, so I've made it through the day. I go directly to my locker, get what I need, walk down the corridor, and suddenly am face to face with Emery Day.

"Hi again," he says quietly, without smiling. "I heard all about the feathers and stuff at lunchtime. That's why I went looking for you. Listen, Robin, you don't need to put up with . . ."

Just then Randi and Michelle and a couple of other kids pass us going the other way. Michelle kind of lags behind, watching me and Emery and smiling — more like smirking, really. Then she catches up with the rest of them and says something and they all laugh. I don't hear her, but I know what she's saying, which is, "Hey, look who Robin's going around with now — that little shrimp Emery Day, for God's sake!" I know that's what they're saying because that's exactly what I would have said.

I can't stand it. I can't stand there thinking I'm that desperate. I may not have any friends, but I still have my pride. Emery's still trying to tell me something, but I don't want anything to do with him. "Listen, Emery," I say, loud enough for all to hear, "do me a huge favor, will you, and just get lost."

I leave Emery standing there looking like someone who has just been punched in the stomach, and then I just get out of there fast and practically run all the way home.

No one is here, and the first thing I see is a huge note from Jamie, stuck on the refrigerator with a stupid magnet in the shape of a cockroach. The note is written with a red marking pen on a full sheet of binder paper: "Call Grandma Noddy right away."

I immediately think something terrible has happened to Muncie. I don't phone. I just run next door and rush in without even knocking.

Muncie is sitting in front of the TV, watching some sort of noisy quiz show. All kinds of lights are flashing and bells are ringing and people are squealing and jumping up and down in crazy animal costumes. Muncie is sitting there munching on something and nodding his head.

I'm so relieved to see he's okay that I go over and hug him, but he's still watching the program and hardly notices me. A second later Grandma Noddy comes in. "Robin! How long have you been here?"

"I just got here. What's wrong? Jamie left a note."

She motions with her head toward the kitchen and I follow her in.

"It's Wink," she says. "You won't believe this, but he tripped over a traffic cop in the street outside his office and fractured his collarbone."

"How did he do that, for heaven's sake?"

"Don't ask me. All I know is that the cop was directing traffic and turned around to blow his whistle and Wink just wasn't watching where he was going."

"Oh boy," I say. "That's awful. But is he okay? I mean, can they — "

"He'll be okay," she breaks in. "They got him to the hospital and I've even talked to him on the phone. He'll be okay."

"Whew." Then I remember. "But your trip! You're supposed to leave day after tomorrow! Oh, Grandma, what are you going to do?"

"That's what Wink wants to talk to you about, Robin. Wink says he's got all the reservations made. He says there's nothing to it. He says you could handle it with no trouble at all."

"*Me? Me?* Handle *what?* You mean me, go with you to Venice? I can't do that! I don't know anything about traveling! Really, Grandma!"

"He's over at City General, Room 418. He wants you to go right over there."

My grandma gives me a wistful little smile. "Come on, Robin. Don't look so shocked. You can do it."

City General Hospital is about three miles away, but

it's right on the bus line. I only have to wait about ten minutes. Once on the bus, I finally begin to realize that I might really go to Venice. And all because of a traffic cop. I wonder what Emery Day would say to that. And then I start to feel lousy; just to save face with a bunch of former friends, I hit on Emery like that. So I'm really a snob, through and through. I'm just like Tracy, selfish and self-centered. Grandmother Boyd has been right all along.

I get off at the hospital and go right to Room 418, but Wink's not there. One of the nurses tells me they've moved him down to 402 and that's where I find him, his shoulder bandaged up like a mummy.

He smiles when he sees me, and I say, "What happened, Uncle Wink? Slip off a barstool again?" It's an old joke.

His roommate, an old guy about eighty, thinks it's hilarious.

"Very funny, Robin," Wink says. "Now, here's the deal. First of all, can you miss some school? Can you miss a week?"

The prospect of missing a week of school sounds like heaven to me. "Sure. How about two weeks?"

Wink ignores my comment. "Well, if it'll help, I'll call Buzz myself and tell him it's an emergency." He squirms around in the bed. "Old Buzz owes me one, anyway. Truthfully, my first thought was Jamie, but he tells me it's impossible. He says he's got a twenty-page research paper to do and it's overdue already."

Wink starts to turn toward me but lies back down with a groan. "There" — he points — "in the closet there. Get the notebook from my coat pocket."

I do as he tells me. "This?" I ask.

"That's it. Now, flip through it — there, toward the back. There's my travel agent's phone number. His name is Gordon. I've already called him and explained what happened. He'll deliver the tickets and all the information to you tomorrow night."

"Okay."

"But take his phone number in case there's any problem."

I tear the page out of the notebook. "Okay."

"Now you're going to have to get a passport."

"Gee, that's right. I didn't even think about that."

"George Watson is going to take care of it. He's a friend of mine from the office. George'll pick you up tomorrow morning at nine and walk you through. Bring your birth certificate. He knows all the ropes, so there shouldn't be any problem."

Wink finally pauses and looks at me. "I know you can handle this, Robin. There's nothing to it. Your grandma will have her hands full watching over Muncie, so you'll be in charge of the details. Here's what's happening. You'll just fly into Rome, take a train to Venice, take a gondola to the hotel, and you're all set. Everybody speaks English. And you'll probably even have a great time. Venice is a beautiful place."

"A *gondola?*" I say. "I can't believe this is really happening."

I notice the old man in the next bed is still smiling at me. All of a sudden I feel so confident and devilish, I just look right back at him and wink my eye, as boldly as you please, and he blushes about fifteen shades of red.

After I leave Wink, I stop at the restroom on the fourth floor for a minute. Then I walk over to the elevator and push the Down button. The elevator light flashes on number 4, the door slides open, and there stands Emery Day with his hands in his pockets and a very surprised look on his face. "Oh, Jesus," he says. "What are *you* doing here?"

I can't move. The door begins to close, and Emery steps forward and quickly pushes a button on the panel, causing the door to open again with a jerk. "Well, are you getting in or not?" he asks forcefully, so I do.

I feel like a fool. I realize right away there's only one thing to do and that's apologize to Emery Day. "I'm really sorry," I say, "for telling you to get lost at school this afternoon. It was really stinking of me."

He looks at me for a second, probably trying to figure out if I'm sincere.

"That's okay," he replies. "I know how it is. You just didn't want to be seen with me right then." Then he adds, "I know all about how your crowd is."

I don't know how to answer that.

We're on the ground floor now. We step out of the elevator, and for a minute I can't remember which way I came in, so I just stand there feeling slightly lost.

Emery seems to sense my uncertainty. "Looking for the door?"

"Yes."

"Everybody gets lost in here. Come this way," he says, and I follow him out of the building.

"Taking the bus?" he asks, and when I nod he says, "Well, you have to catch it around the corner. Come on. I'll walk over there with you. Unless, of course, you're embarrassed to be seen with me," he mocks.

Something in the tone of his voice really gets to me. I stop walking and turn to look at him. He has turned his shirt collar up against the chill of the late afternoon, and his usually pale complexion looks almost bruised by a sudden cold breeze that whips around the corner of the building.

"Emery," I say, surprised at the almost tender feeling I have for him, "I told you I was sorry, and I meant it."

I'm looking into his dark blue eyes now, and I can't turn away. He's the one who finally drops his gaze and starts walking again.

"Hey, Robin," he says after a moment, as if we've been pals for years, "do you know Bryon Sweeney? He's on the wrestling team."

"I know who he is. Why?"

"Well, last summer he and I drove up to San Francisco to visit his aunt and uncle for a couple of days, and while we were there, his aunt's high school class had their thirty-fifth reunion and she went to it. When she got home, do you know what she said to us?"

"What?"

"She said, 'You know, boys, believe it or not, some of those little snots I went to high school with have finally turned into really nice human beings.' "

That strikes me so funny, I laugh outright.

I sit down on the bench at the bus stop and Emery sits beside me.

"So, what are you doing at the hospital?" I ask.

"Oh, I come over here two afternoons a week. I'm a volunteer."

"You are? Doing what?"

"Lots of stuff. Whatever they want. A bunch of us come. Do you know Delores Sweeney? She's Bryon's cousin. She comes, and Vicki Frazier . . ."

So that's the Vicki who left the message for him, I think.

"Here comes number twenty-three. Is that your bus?" he asks.

"Yes. Aren't you getting on?"

He stands up and shakes his head. Then he checks his watch. "I get a ride at five-thirty with some of the others."

"Oh," I say, wondering how come Emery has friends I don't even know about.

The bus is stopped across the street at a red light now. "Hey, Emery," I say just as the light changes to green and the bus heads toward us. "Guess what? You'll love this. If I hadn't have stopped off at the restroom before getting on the elevator, I would have missed you. What do you think of that?"

"Not much," he says, and although he tries to hide it, I know he's amused.

13

My uncle trips over a traffic cop in Los Angeles, so here I am, halfway across the world in Venice, Italy. We've been here for two days and Grandma Noddy has put the final touches on her novel. To celebrate, the three of us go out for some gelato in a sidewalk café downstairs. We're all wearing long wool socks and thick sweaters and feel quite warm in spite of the cool afternoon. The young waiter we have come to know smiles at us and asks in English if we'd rather go inside, indicating with a sweep of his arm that there are plenty of seats indoors.

Grandma Noddy shakes her head. No, she would rather have it out here, where she can see the water.

"Very well." The waiter smiles and takes out his pad and pencil. Grandma Noddy motions to me, so I do the ordering. "We'd like three espressos and three gelatos, please," I say.

We don't speak as we wait for our coffee and ice cream.

The past two days I have been taking Muncie outdoors for an hour or two each afternoon while my grandma finished her last chapter. The Italians would nod and smile knowingly at the two of us as we slowly made our way to our favorite spot in St. Mark's Square. We would sit in the sunshine until we were warm, watching the pigeons in the square and the shadows beginning to fall across the beautiful old church opposite us. A pair of young lovers once strolled by in front of us, and I found myself thinking about the movie I saw with Emery and the feeling of the wind blowing my hair as we rode back home on his bike.

The waiter soon returns with our order, and I move my chair closer to Muncie, hovering over him slightly, silently signaling to my grandma that I will watch over him this time. He soon begins to make a mess of it, so I end up feeding him little spoonfuls while my grandma gazes at the Grand Canal, her eyes brimming with tears.

The portions are small, and in a few minutes we are finished.

"Good, Grandfather," I say. "You did a good job with that."

In the pause that follows, I can hear the echo of those words from out of the past, and now I'm a tiny child, and I'm the one being helped with my ice cream, and my grandfather is saying to me, "Good. You did a good job with that."

I look at him now, wondering if he will remember how he once said those words to me, but it is much too late for that. After a while, we go for the last time and sit at our table in the sunshine of St. Mark's Square.

It is night. From our hotel we hear singing down below on the canal. We shut off the lights in our room and swing open our large wooden shutters. The moonlight is shining on the dark rippling water as the gondolas glide smoothly under the bridge.

"Oh," Grandma whispers, "it is beautiful beyond description. It's more than I ever dreamed. Oh, Muncie, isn't that the most thrilling sight you've ever seen?"

I look over at my grandfather. He's slumped in his chair, his eyes staring vacantly in the dim light. He's fumbling with his pipe, trying to light it with what appears to be his comb.

I swallow several times, but the lump just won't go away. Finally, I wave my hand in the soft Venice air and reach over and touch my grandfather's cheek. "Ehh," I whisper for him, like a farewell lullaby. "Ehh, just gondolas, and moonlight."

After we get Muncie to bed, Grandma returns to the window to watch the canal, and I know she wants to be alone. I go to the café downstairs and sit by myself at an inside table. Our waiter is still on duty.

"Ah," he says, smiling and walking up to me. "It is the young lady from California."

"Now, how did you know that?" I ask, folding my arms and leaning on the small table.

He draws up a chair and straddles it backward. He is a handsome young Italian, and he is flirting with me.

"Very simple." He winks. "I tell that by the way you speak."

"Oh," I say, trying not to blush.

"The old man," the waiter says, motioning as if he is feeding ice cream to me, "the old man, he is your grandfather?"

I nod. "Yes. My grandfather."

"Ah, you are so beautiful with him. You love him very much."

A couple at a nearby table are waving at the waiter now, the man raising his arms and swinging them like a windmill.

"Oh, excuse me, pardon me just a moment, please," he says to me and saunters over to them.

You love him very much, the waiter said. There is something about that phrase. You love him very much. Why does it stay in my mind? Why does it seem to strike some discordant note? I do love him very much. Of course I do.

But wait. Now I hear another theme. Tracy. Tracy didn't love anyone. Selfish and self-centered. That's what they said about Tracy. So, I am *not* like her. I am not like Tracy after all.

The waiter is returning, holding my espresso at arm's length, showing off for me.

"I am not like my aunt Tracy," I say to him, and he cocks his head and shrugs and says, "Okay."

"We are leaving tomorrow," I tell him, and he nods sadly.

"But you will return someday. You will return someday with the boy you love," he says, because he is Italian, and all Italians are romantic.

We've been on the plane for over six hours, and everyone is tired. My grandfather has been sleeping fitfully for most of that time, and my grandma is looking very old.

I have been thinking about the world. I leave my seat from time to time and walk about the plane and look closely at my fellow passengers, sprawled on the seats in human disarray. In one sudden insight, as sharp and clear as the blue, blue sky surrounding me, I realize that Southside High is but an insignificant speck in the vastness of the universe. Oh, joy. I am free at last.

14

I hear about Emery Day's surprising plan to run for the office of Spring Semester Student Body President on my first day back at school. Mrs. Carrothers is reading the announcement bulletin during first period and says that all candidates for student offices must turn in their petitions, signed by at least one hundred students, by three o'clock that afternoon and be ready to present their nomination skits at the assembly next Monday. After Mrs. Carrothers lets her glasses fall (they are hanging by a gold chain around her neck), George Davis raises his hand and asks permission to circulate a petition for Emery. Some of the kids laugh, especially Michelle and Jennifer. Mrs. Carrothers says that will be permissible as long as it's put away in exactly (she checks her wrist-watch) four minutes and thirty-two seconds. Then Jennifer quickly raises her hand. She announces that she's

Marla Peters's campaign manager and she wants to circulate a petition on Marla's behalf. *So, I think, she's finally thought of something spectacular to do.* Jennifer looks over at George Davis and says in her best intimidating manner, "Why don't you just forget it, Georgie? Emery doesn't have a prayer."

Student body elections are such a big farce at my school. For one thing, the officers have about as much power to change things as a stray cat in a Laundromat; for another thing, the fact that they have no power doesn't even matter, since the kinds of people who are elected never want to change anything anyway. It's just a big, overrated popularity contest. I wonder why in the world a person like Emery Day would even consider running. Marla Peters, the white-haired sex goddess, surely has it all signed, sealed and delivered, anyway.

I spend all my lunch hours in the library now, and hardly mind it at all. Besides, I have lots of work to make up — a report on *The Scarlet Letter*, a chapter outline for History, and an essay for that big jerk Mr. Alex Huntsman on the dramatic potential of *As You Like It*.

Some of the time I just sit there, staring at my books and papers, worrying about what's happening to Muncie. After we returned from Venice, he seemed to go straight downhill. He flatly refused to be helped with his food any longer, even slapping a spoon to the ground and throwing a cup of milk against the wall. Grandma Noddy had a conference with Dad and Wink, and they decided that he had become more than she could handle. So now he's in a convalescent home, still refusing every attempt at help from anyone. Yesterday he yanked out the intravenous feeding tube, and Grandma Noddy and Dad and Wink are supposed to have a meeting with Dr. Morris today to discuss what to do next. I don't think they should do anything. Muncie kept his promise about Venice (as best he could), and now I think he just wants to die. More than anything else, Muncie's whole illness has made me realize how really fleeting life is.

Wink is out of the hospital now, but he hasn't gone back to work, at least not to the office. I think he's finishing up the novel about Lark Greenwillow, because last night he asked me if kids ever dance "slow dances" anymore and if they still say "going all the way."

It's Thursday night, and I just got a phone call I think may change my life. It was from Delores Sweeney. Like her cousin Bryon Sweeney, I know who she is, but we've never spoken to each other. She was calling to ask me if I would consider being a volunteer at the hospital. She said I could start tomorrow afternoon. Actually, we had quite a long conversation. She said she and Vicki Frazier volunteer because they want to be nurses, but most of the other kids just volunteer because they want to. She also mentioned that she was the person who recruited Emery. She happened to see him at the hospital one day when he was there with his mother, who's getting cancer therapy. She said she knew him because he was a good friend of Bryon's, and she just thought he might like to be a volunteer. Then she said if it was okay, she'd meet me by the drinking fountain in the cafeteria at noon tomorrow, and they could tell me all about it. I was so excited about being asked, I had a hard time trying not to sound like an overjoyed maniac. I'm almost certain Emery put her up to it.

I've eaten in the cafeteria for years, but I've never seemed to notice that the other kids there are just as alive and breathing as my former "little group," as my mother would say. After standing by the drinking fountain with my tray for several minutes (and almost beginning to panic), I see Delores Sweeney hurrying up to me.

"Gosh, I'm sorry I'm late, Robin," she says. "I forgot my purse in English and had to go all the way back for it."

"That's okay," I say.

"We usually sit over there," she says. "Come on."

I walk right past the table full of double-A tens. The only person who acknowledges me as I go by is Muriel Monroe.

Delores and I make our way to a table in the corner of the cafeteria. Then she introduces me to Vicki Frazier and another girl named Ann Something-or-other. Emery Day and Bryon Sweeney and some other guys are sitting there, too. Of course, I've seen all of them around and have even had classes with some of them, but I don't really know them. Emery is talking to George Davis as I sit down, and although he doesn't interrupt himself to say anything to me out loud, he welcomes me with his eyes and a nod of his head.

The talk around the table is not about the hospital,

however, but about Emery's candidacy for president. Ann tells me quietly that the reason he's running is that his mother, who's dying of cancer, told Vicki Frazier at the hospital that Emery's father was president of his high school student body back in a little town in Oklahoma (where they had gone to school together), and if he were alive, it would make him wildly happy to see his son following in his footsteps, or something like that.

I don't say anything, of course, but I think how stupid and unfair it is for people to expect kids to be like their parents, and I think it's really sad when all parents have to look forward to is some sort of accomplishment like that on the part of their kids. I suppose, though, that an exception can be made in a case like Emery's mother.

"And then," Ann adds softly, "being elected president couldn't exactly hurt as far as his chances for getting a scholarship are concerned. He wants to be a pediatrician, you know."

That's news to me. "He does?" I ask.

She nods and smiles. "He told me once that pediatricians *should* be short, like their patients, so they can sneak up on the little rug rats with their loaded hypodermics."

Now everyone's listening to Bryon. "What you really need, Em," he's saying, "is some sort of election *gimmick*. Something that'll get the kids who never bother to vote over to the polls. You know, kids like us."

That's the first time I ever heard anyone call Emery "Em." I like the sound of it.

Everyone around the table pauses to consider Bryon's idea about a gimmick, and George Davis makes some sort of stupid suggestion, an impossible idea involving a helicopter or something. Well, apparently it strikes Emery funny, because he suddenly burst out laughing in such an honest, lovable way, I can't help staring at him. Then his eyes catch mine and hold them, and something extraordinary and miraculous takes place: I have another PIP. This time, a former first-class gold medal nobody is transformed into a dream, and I suddenly realize that the boy an Italian waiter told me I would someday like to return to Venice with is a beak-nosed little red-headed guy named Emery Day.

That afternoon, five of us meet after school and Bryon Sweeney takes us in his car to City General. They put me on the geriatric floor and it almost kills me at first, since a few of the people there remind me so much of Muncie. Thank God there are some others who are really sharp and truly want to go on living.

The first lady I help is ninety-two years old. I help her write a letter to her boyfriend, who's eighty-seven. In the next room I ask an old guy if there's anything I can do for him, and he says there certainly is. He would like me to toss out the flowers on his bedside table. He's a real grouch, and says he doesn't understand why his harebrained daughter insists on wasting money on stinking flowers every time he's in the hospital and then is always wanting to borrow money from him as soon as he gets home. I don't throw the flowers away; they're much too pretty for that. I just take them to the next room and ask the two ladies there if they would like them, which they would. The TV is on softly, although neither woman seems to be really watching it. It seems to be a program of black and white comedy shorts from the old days. It looks like the Three Stooges or Abbott and Costello, but anyway, everyone is throwing pies around. First one guy gets it, then the other, and finally an innocent bystander is slapped full in the face with a huge cream pie. From one of the hospital beds comes a kind of gurgling laughter, soon answered by a lively cackle from the other side of the room.

Something clicks in my brain, and on the way home in the car I quietly ask Emery if he can stop by my house tomorrow (Saturday), as I think I have the idea of the century, an idea that can probably get him elected president of the student body in a landslide.

"Okay, here's my plan," I say to Emery. It was his idea that we ride over to the Burger King on his bicycle, and now we're sitting at the same table where we sat on Christmas Day. He's watching me with amused skepticism as we wait for our cheeseburgers and fries.

"You'll need some tall girl to help you out, see," I begin, "and she wears a white wig and maybe a T-shirt that says MARLA."

"This is for the skit assembly, right?" he asks.

"Right. The skit. So you and the Marla look-alike get in some sort of squabble, and she ends up hitting you in the face with a pie."

"In the face with a pie," he repeats. "I see. Go ahead."

"And then *you* pick up a pie, intending to hit her

back, only — and this is the part that still needs some polishing — by some mistake or other you miss Marla, and instead you hit . . ."

"Yes?" He smiles. "I hit . . ."

"Mr. Bussone."

"And get expelled from school," he adds quickly. "It's a brilliant idea, Robin, but I'm afraid it has one fatal flaw."

"I can take care of Mr. Bussone," I say. "Trust me. Other than that, what do you think?"

Emery stares off into space and slowly begins to nod his head. "Other than that," he mutters. "Hmm. Vote for the guy who hit the Buzzard with the pie. Pass it on," he whispers. "A great word-of-mouth campaign. Lordy, that *is* great. Impossible, but great."

"You really think it would get all those deadbeats to the polls?"

"Oh, no doubt about it," he says. "If it comes down to a choice between Marla Peters and the guy who hit the Buzzard with the pie, there'd be no contest. Gee, I can hear them roaring now as the Buzzard stands there, whipped cream running down his face. But let's be realistic, Robin. Mr. Bussone would kill me right on the stage. He'd splatter me all over the curtains and sweep up the remains with a whiskbroom."

"Em," I say, "don't worry about Mr. Bussone. You'll see. You've heard about the proverbial ace in the hole? Well, that's what I've got — a big fat ace in the hole."

"I sure hope so," he says, "but I'll believe it when I see it."

I have to go to the bathroom. "Listen," I say, standing up, "I'm going to go wash my hands."

"Okay," he says, reaching for a newspaper that someone had left behind. "I'll watch for our order."

When I come out of the restroom, Emery's sitting at the table with our tray in front of him, reading the classified section of the *Times*.

"Did you know that people can communicate with the dead?" he asks, pushing my cheeseburger over to me.

I look at Emery's face, but I'm thinking about Bill. I'm thinking about what a boring conversationalist Bill really is.

"Listen to this," Emery continues. "It's in the In Memoriam column." He clears his throat and reads. "To David Allen, passed away to be with Our Lord seven years ago today. We miss you very much, David, and will always love you. Grandma sends her love, too. Signed, Mom, Dad, and Bernie." Emery puts the paper down and starts to unwrap his cheeseburger. "I sure hope they deliver the *Times* in the Great Beyond."

I don't answer. I think what he just read is so sad I can't stand it. We eat in silence for a few minutes. Then I say, "You know, on the plane back from Venice I was thinking about what you told me before, you know, about how you thought the fear of death was the main reason for religion."

"That's very profound," he replies, furrowing his brow. "Did I really say that?"

"I think it was you," I retort. "It was either you or this four-year-old I baby-sit for sometimes. But anyway," I

182

continue, "seriously, what I've been thinking is that I don't think it's the fear of death that makes people religious as much as it is . . . love."

"Love?"

"When I think about my grandfather, for instance, well, I just think people have religion because they can't bear the thought of losing people they love."

Emery's eyes seem to moisten. "Could be," he says finally. "I don't know. I just think it makes more sense to try to do all you can for people who are still alive and try not to dwell too much on" — he hesitates and looks away — "on the dead."

"Is that why you want to be a doctor?" I ask quietly.

He blushes suddenly. "Who told you that?"

"Oh, somebody at school."

"Well, they're wrong. I want to be a doctor so I can make a bundle before I'm forty-five and then retire to Miami Beach." The only thing that gives him away is the slight lifting of his left eyebrow combined with a barely perceptible hint of a smile.

"Oh, *right*," I say, beginning to love his style more and more every second.

An hour later we're in Wink's little front room and I'm revealing my ace in the hole.

"So that's the story," I say, after explaining my idea to Wink. "What do you think? Do you want to collect that debt and help Emery get elected student body president?"

"I love it!" Wink exclaims, rubbing his hands together. "My God. A pie! Talk about poetic justice!" And then he explains how Mr. Bussone once bribed another student to let Wink himself have it with a pie in the face just as he was about to pick up his date at her dorm. "This guy comes at me from behind and taps me on the shoulder just as poor Barbie opened her door."

"Why did he do that?" I ask. "Just for fun?"

Wink smiles. "Oh, I don't know. Unless, uh, unless it had something to do with Buzz's missing pants." He laughs now. "It's a long story."

"Those were the days, huh?" Emery says, with just the right amount of humorously feigned enthusiasm.

Wink shakes his head from side to side. "You'd better believe it, son. You'd better believe it."

Then he opens his wallet and fishes out the old note from Mr. James "Buzz" Bussone. "Hand me the phone book there," he says to me. "I haven't talked to the old boy for years."

I'm not too surprised to learn that Mr. Bussone's address is not listed in the directory. He's much too smart for that. The only likely listing is simply a "J. Bussone," and a phone number.

Wink dials the number, and Emery and I exchange knowing smiles as he says, "Buzz? Guess who this is, you old so-and-so." He laughs and jokes for a few minutes and then asks if he can "come over for a short visit." He adds, "I've got a little piece of paper here I want to collect on." He smiles and gives us the pilot's thumbs-up sign. "Right! You remember it, huh?" He gets the address and then he says, "And, oh, listen, I'm bringing my niece along, and a friend of hers. Okay? See you soon, then."

15

Well, Mr. Bussone agreed to get smacked with a pie (he turned out to be a really neat guy), and Emery Day was elected student body president by a whopping three-to-one majority. He'll probably get that scholarship now, too. Bill and Jennifer, of course, were chosen as the King and Queen of Hearts.

Mr. Bussone was outside, clipping his hedge, that Saturday afternoon as Wink, Emery and I drove up to his house. Two of his boys were tossing a Frisbee all over the neighborhood, and a third was playing with a puppy inside the walled-in porch. Mrs. Bussone, dressed in old jeans and a sweatshirt, was raking up the hedge clippings. She invited us in for cookies and chocolate and said with a sweet smile that she had always wanted to meet the hero who had saved her husband's life.

We stayed for over two hours. Mr. Bussone built a fire

in the fireplace and told us of his plans and dreams for Southside High.

His strategy was to spend the first several years getting the kids back in line. "Truthfully now," he asked, leveling his gaze at me and Emery, "haven't conditions improved since you two were freshmen?"

"Well," Emery began, "those rowdy gangs have been broken up."

"Exactly," Mr. Bussone agreed, taking his youngest child on his lap.

"I hear the neighbors around the school have finally quit sending petitions to the school board," Wink added.

"The kids are really settling down," Mr. Bussone said. "When I took that job, it was like a jungle over there." He smoothed down his child's hair and tenderly put him on the couch beside him. "Now, little by little, I'll start giving some privileges back. There are a lot of good kids in that school."

Later, Wink broached the subject of the pie. Mr. Bussone was great. He acted as though he had no other choice; he had said he would do anything, and, by God, he would. We worked out the details of the skit right then and there. After the Marla look-alike got Emery with her pie, Emery would turn around to land one on her. That's when Mr. Bussone would step forward from behind the curtain, ostensibly to put a stop to the pie throwing, and Marla would duck and — whammo! We even gave the skit a dry run, with me playing Marla, and it really looked good. Emery said that maybe the "whipped cream" would really be shaving cream, and Mrs. Bussone laughed and said he'd wear an old suit that day, and she would be there in the back of the auditorium with her movie camera.

When we left, Mr. Bussone shook Emery's hand and said that he didn't know who else was running for president, but that he'd had his eye on Emery for a long time, and he was certain that if he were elected he'd do a great job, and he wished him lots of luck.

The two older boys flanked their dad as we turned to leave. They had been quiet throughout our visit, but now they started to horse around, pantomiming some pie throwing as their mother good-naturedly tried to calm them down. "All right, boys," she said, and Mr. Bussone playfully grabbed the nearest one by the ear. The impression I got was that this was one of the nicest, most loving families I had ever seen.

As we headed for the car, Mr. Bussone stepped down off the porch and waved good-bye. "It was great to see you, Wink," he called out. "Come by again, will you? We'll rehash the old days!"

"Righto!" Wink called back, and we drove off down the street.

Spring semester is under way at Southside High, and I'm out of Mr. Huntsman's class (thank God) and now have a class that period called Psychology for Everyday Life. The instructor, Mr. Peak, is an older guy with a black beard.

Mr. Peak writes his name on the board and tells us that he came into the teaching profession relatively late in life. For ten years he was a practicing psychologist specializing in the rehabilitation of alcoholics. He shared his office with a man named Milton Seymour.

"Peak and Seymour, it said on our door," he tells us. "A lot of people thought we were a detective agency."

I look around the room as the class laughs at that, and, to my surprise, I see a boy wearing a Levi's vest, and it is not Emery Day.

Mr. Peak starts giving us a little preview of what we're going to study. He says the first unit will be about heredity and environment, and how each contributes to the fabric of our lives.

Along with heredity and environment, I think we should also study *chance*. I think we should study little pieces of dust, and walnut shells in banana nut bread, because when you stop and think about it, those are the kinds of things that really end up changing lives. On an impulse, I raise my hand and say that to Mr. Peak. He's pretty nice about it. He just thinks about it for a few seconds and says in a friendly way, "Well now, that's an odd thought, isn't it?" I know I'm going to like this class.

This is one of my hospital days, so after school I go out to the parking lot to wait for Bryon Sweeney and the other kids. While I'm waiting, I notice Muriel Monroe walking by. She's not with any of the old gang. Instead, she's with some girls from the Latin Club, a brainy group that meets unofficially before school every morning with old Mrs. Vanderguth. Muriel sees me, excuses herself, and rushes over to my side. The other kids stop and wait for her.

"I want to call you tonight," she says breathlessly. "I've got so much to tell you!"

I nod and smile at her, and we hug each other briefly. She starts to leave, then turns halfway back to me and calls over her shoulder, "It's not so bad after all, is it, Robin, being in with the out crowd?"

And I answer proudly, not caring who hears me, "No, no, a million times no!"

I'm not sure if Emery is coming with us today or not. His new responsibilities as student body president are taking up more and more of his free time. Even though I have come to see Emery in a new light, so to speak, there seems to be no great change in his attitude toward me, which might be described as cautious friendship.

I make up my mind, out here in the parking lot, that I am going to ask him to the King and Queen of Hearts Dance. I want to be seen publicly, at a school dance, with Emery Day. I think he would probably like to ask me but isn't sure I'd accept. I feel strangely elated by this idea. I can almost sense his appreciation and gratitude.

Emery does show up, and at the hospital we're assigned to work in the small gift shop. He has done that job before and I am to learn it today.

Business is slow. (We sell several magazines and one stuffed buffalo.) So I decide that now is the time. I sit on the stool next to the cash register and nonchalantly play with the keys. Emery is straightening out the candy bar rack just beside me.

"Ever been to a King and Queen of Hearts Dance?" I ask lightly.

"Nope." I think I see his eyes flicker.

"Would you like to go with me?" It comes out so smoothly; there is nothing to it.

"Oh, gee, Robin," he says, "I'm sorry, but I've already got a date."

I look up quickly. "You *have?*"

"Yeah. I'm going with Vicki Frazier."

I feel my cheeks flush, and he mercifully turns away from me, but not soon enough to hide a hint of smugness I think I detect in his face.

An overweight nurse walks up and asks him for an Idaho Spud candy bar. He takes her money (the exact change) and watches over my shoulder as I work the register. I feel like punching him right in the nose.

Emery has been extra nice to me all week. Yesterday he asked if he could appoint me to the Finance Committee. All they do is check up on the treasurer's reports and okay expenditures, so I said, "I don't care. I'll do it if you can't find anyone else," and then I walked away.

Now it's Friday. Tonight's the big dance. However, not only am I not the Queen of Hearts, I'm not even going to be there!

Emery comes to my locker after school and asks if I'm going right home.

"I guess so," I answer. "Why?"

"I just wanted to walk along, if you don't mind."

I shrug. "Oh, okay." I wonder if maybe Vicki is sick and he wants me to go with him after all.

We walk along silently for almost a block. I'm determined to let him speak first, and finally he does. "I'm sorry about the dance tonight."

I just keep walking. So Vicki is not sick.

"Vicki and I have been friends for a long time," he says.

"Oh, yeah?"

He suddenly takes my hand. It's the first time he's ever touched me like that, deliberately. He stops walking and we look at each other. "It doesn't mean anything," he says. "It's no big romance or anything."

"Great." I wonder if he can see the blood vessels in my neck pounding.

Emery's got a giant pimple on his nose today. It looks really ridiculous. His nose is big anyway, for his face, and it looks terrible. But I don't dwell on it, even though it hurts me. It hurts me just as if it were on my own nose.

We're walking again now. We're passing the shopping center, and I can see our reflection in the store windows. I wonder why I've never noticed before how he walks with a certain grace and sureness.

He's still holding my hand and he's giving little signals — two weak squeezes and a strong, two strongs and three weaks, and on like that.

"Know Morse Code?" he asks.

"No. What are you signaling?"

"I don't know. I don't know it, either," he says, and we laugh. Everything seems right between us now.

In a few minutes we're passing the Burger King. "Let's stop," he says.

We get some Cokes and of course we take them to our usual table. I know something is on his mind. He keeps looking at me, almost saying something, but then he doesn't.

We sit in silence for a while until he says, "So how was Venice? You haven't told me about your trip yet."

"Words cannot describe it," I say. "It's one of those places you have to see to believe."

He nods. "That's what I've heard. I'd really like to go there someday."

I'm beginning to think he can actually read my mind.

"And your grandfather?" he asks quietly. "How is he doing?"

"Not good. Really not good."

"I'm sorry. I shouldn't have asked."

I shake my head. "No. That's okay." But I have to blink to keep the tears away. "What's it all about, anyway?" I ask suddenly. "You're born, you lead a good life, and then you slowly lose your mind. So what's life all about? Is there really any purpose?"

"Why ask me?" he answers gently. "I sure don't have the answer."

"You're student body president, aren't you?" I ask, realizing the conversation is heading toward a dead end and attempting to change the mood.

He shrugs in a self-depreciating way. "Thanks to you."

After a long moment he touches my arm. "Robin, the Senior Ball is in May. I'd really like you to go with me. How about it?"

I look at him for a long time. I look deep into those beautiful blue, moist, red-rimmed eyes and I wonder how I can tell him yes in a style all our own. And then it begins to come to me. Not only can I tell him yes, but, at the same time (if I do it properly), I can also exorcise all of his superficial shortcomings forever.

By affecting a barely imperceptible hint of a smile and a slight lifting of my left eyebrow, I try to imitate the way he looked when he told me that bold-faced lie about wanting to be a doctor just for the money.

"Emery," I say, gambling all I have on the hope that he'll understand exactly what I'm trying to do, "Emery, I won't even consider going to the Senior Ball with you until your face clears up and you grow at least six inches." I want to say something about his big nose too, to get it out in the open and let him know I accept him just as he is, but on such short notice I can't manage it all.

Emery stares at me, shocked, for just an instant, then he smiles broadly and slowly takes my hands in his. He leans across the table and kisses me on the lips. "I knew you'd say yes," he whispers, "but isn't there something you forgot to mention?"

He takes out his pen and starts to write on his napkin. He writes painstakingly, in huge spirally letters, and surrounds them with question marks. He stops often to contemplate and admire his work, all the while partially hiding it from my view.

Finally, he looks at it for one last time. "That's it," he says. "I've got the answer to your question," he explains. "The answer to your question about the meaning and purpose of life."

He folds the napkin and slides it across the table to me. I open it, and here's what I see:

The phone rings at about six that evening. I'm helping Naomi with her homework. Actually, I'm not really helping; I'm just trying to do what Grandma Noddy did for me, and that's looking over Naomi's papers from yesterday and being interested in her good work. I tell her we're sure going to surprise Mom when report card time comes. I think of it as contributing positively to Naomi's environment.

It's Emery on the phone. "There's a message for you in your mailbox," he says. "It's just something that occurred to me after I saw you today."

"Okay. I'll go get it."

"Well, I guess that's all I had to say right now."

"Emery?"

"Yeah?"

"Don't have too much fun at the dance tonight."

There's a long pause. I hear him take a breath. "Good-bye, Robin," he says.

I go out to the mailbox and find the letter. It feels at least three pages thick. I take it to my room and shut the door. Then I sit on my bed and tear open the envelope. It's not a letter at all but several sheets of thin tissue paper secured by a paper clip. I unwrap it carefully and my breath catches, for lying there in the tissue paper are the crumpled remains of a dead bee.

Early in the evening Wink brings over his completed manuscript for me to read, in which Lark Greenwillow becomes the Queen of Hearts in 150 pages by saying no to all of the boys. If it's fantasy Wink was after, he certainly achieved it.

After finishing the novel, I slip the thick rubber band back around the manuscript and look at my watch. It's only a little after eleven. I don't want to go to bed yet because I have a feeling Emery will call me after the dance, probably to tell me that he's fallen madly in love with Vicki Frazier. And I'll tell him that's okay, since Prince Charles has just phoned from London to tell me he's willing to give up everything for me. And then — oh, God, I get to feeling weak all over just thinking about it — Emery may put his lips close to the phone and whisper something very, very sweet.

Just to help pass the time, and because it's been on my mind, I borrow some of Mom's best stationery and write a letter to good old Prince Charles. This is what I say:

Dear Prince Charles:
I recently read an article about you in which you are quoted as saying that you sometimes wonder, out of all the people you could have been, you happened to be born the first son of the Queen of England and, thus, the future King. If that article is true, and if that is what you really said, I want to tell you that I know exactly how you feel, because I sort of wonder the same thing. Out of all the people in the world, I wonder, how did I happen to be born the one who would fall in love with a short red-headed boy with a big nose named Emery Day?
Best wishes,
Robin Tweedy-Boyd

I take a long time writing the letter because I want it neat and perfect. Then I get *Little Women* from my room and go sit in the big chair by the phone. It should ring just about any second now.

FLARE ◆ NOVELS
FROM BESTSELLING AUTHOR
NORMA KLEIN

AVON FLARE ◆ NOVELS
FROM BESTSELLING AUTHOR
MARILYN SACHS

BABY SISTER　　　　　**70358-0/$2.50 US/$3.25 Can**
Her sister was everything Penny could never be, until
Penny found something else.

FOURTEEN　　　　　**69842-0/$2.75 US/$3.50 Can**
Rebecca's mother has just finished her fourteenth book.
They'd all been about Rebecca. This time Mrs. Cooper
thought she had played it safe by writing *First Love*, a
typical teenage romance. But that was before Jason
moved next door.

CLASS PICTURES　　　　　**61408-1/$2.75 US/$3.50 Can**
Best friends through thick and thin, until everything
changes in eighth grade, when Lolly suddenly turns into
a thin pretty blonde and Pat, an introspective science
whiz, finds herself playing second fiddle for the first
time.

AV⦿N Paperbacks

AVON FLARE BESTSELLERS

by BRUCE AND CAROLE HART

SOONER OR LATER   42978-0/$2.95US/$3.75Can
Thirteen-year-old Jessie is a romantic and ready for
her first love. She knows that if she's patient, the *real*
thing is bound to happen. And it does, with Michael—
handsome, charming and seventeen!

WAITING GAMES   79012-2/$2.95US/$3.75Can
Michael and Jessie's story continues as they learn what
being in love really means. How much are they willing
to share together—if their love is to last forever?

and a new romance

BREAKING UP IS HARD TO DO
                     89970-1/$2.95US/$3.95Can
Julie and Sean don't know each other, but they have
one big thing in common—they both are falling in love
for the first time...and they're about to learn there's a
world of difference between first love and lasting love.